BAITED

BAITED

An Espionage Thriller

Victoria Montes

ISBN: 0-9798618-3-7
ISBN-13: 978-0-9798618-3-3

To all those who have lost their way.

TABLE OF CONTENTS

The Attack

Some days being a teacher sucked. Third period, I gave James a referral to the principal because he wouldn't sit down. Later, I fretted that I could have been grading the stack of chaotic papers on my desk during my student-free prep period but—I pinched the bridge of my nose—I needed a cold Dr. Pepper.

The afternoon sun beat down on the linoleum floor as I opened the refrigerator to the blast of cooled air, and my fingers wrapped around one of my six cans. The rat-a-tat-tat of an AK-47 pierced the air as my hand slipped from the cool metal, and on reflex, I dove low for cover.

From under one of the tables in the empty lounge, I watched the dark, sugary soda explode from a pin-size puncture in the can due to its collision with the floor.

Settle down. You're not in Afghanistan. You're home, safe. My breath heaved from my chest, and I willed my heart to calm down. You're home. You're safe.

Embarrassed, I jumped up and grabbed the can, rewarded only with a painted face of soda. That is when I heard the screams and more ta-ta-ta-ta-ta of semiautomatic gunfire. I turned. The staff lounge door hung ajar.

I'd heard gunfire four years earlier, and I'd been the first on the scene when an IED—an improvised explosive device- took out one of our convoys. I'd felt helpless then as I watched a pimply faced soldier barely out of his teens trapped in the Humvee, which burst into flames before I could reach it. That must be it. I imagined it. Post-traumatic stress disorder. PTSD—four little letters for years of waking in a cold sweat.

Humorless laughter tickled my throat. Rap music. Stupid, worried over nothing. Music, that's all. I should go tell them to turn it down. But why is my hand shaking? As if to shatter all illusions, thick-tongued words echoed in the distance. The words "Allahu Akbar" were shouted over and over. Machine gun fire shook the walls. Male voices.

I rushed to the door. We'd had drills to prepare for an emergency, but this was real. Across the hall, Mr. Mackee in the biology lab craned his neck around his door as if it were a shield. Then he shrugged and gave me a "What the hell?" look. His eyes widened as more gunshots pierced the air. He darted his head back and slammed the door. I heard a click as the lock slid in place.

I gritted my teeth, sticking my head out to see down the hallway. I half expected to see flames and blackened faces burned beyond recognition. But instead, two students ducked into a room down the hall. "Men with guns," they shouted.

Should I run across the hall, bang on Mackee's door, and help him get the kids out? We could try to escape out the window. A scream and more gunplay made me freeze. My leaden feet wouldn't move across the hallway. Sweat beaded on my forehead, and I couldn't breathe.

But I had to move. Heavy boots resounded from somewhere down the hallway. Banging doors. Stomping, yelling, crying. Gunshots and deadly silence.

I eased the door shut and locked it. I leaned my back against it a moment but then I imagined bullets ripping through it. I jumped up. With a locked door, they'd know someone was in the room. I raced for the window.

The parking lot stretched out two floors below. Half a dozen students ran out toward cars as I pushed the window up. A gun fired, and one of the students dropped to her knees. The others screamed and took off running. I ducked under the windowsill. Oh, no, no, no, no. They're shooting kids.

My hands danced like a wind up toy as I snatched up my cell phone. I pressed 9-1-1. "What's your emergency?" a female dispatcher asked.

I gasped, unable to catch my breath. "I...I... I... they're... they're shooting up our school."

"Okay, ma'am, slow down. Who is shooting?"

"I don't know. I tried to get away, but in the parking lot, they just shot her."

"I'll get you some help. Stay with me. Where are you?"

"Monroe High School."

More screams and more gunfire. They sounded closer.

"First thing is to remain calm and get to a secure place."

I bit my lip to avoid crying. "I'm sorry. This can't happen. I can't stop it. I'm sorry."

I covered my ears with the next series of screams. The phone was pressed to one ear, and the operator asked, "Miss?"

"Sorry. I'm here. There is no secure place."

"Don't be sorry. Can you find a good place to hide? I'll stay with you."

I scanned the room. "Not the closet, they will look there, but I can try the cupboard." Shaking, I bent and threw open one of the sliding panels. Two jars of gold colored glitter sat alone on the shelf. I grabbed them and then shoved my way, feet first, into the bottom shelving. A momentary flash of men imprisoned in a burning Humvee made me almost wriggle out again. Steady your breath. You can do this. Fleeing feet and pulsating gunfire sounded closer.

"They're coming. They'll hear you," I told the dispatcher.

"Take me off speaker but keep the phone on with the volume low."

My finger jabbed at the off button for the speaker twice before connecting as the phone jerked in my sweaty palm. I stuffed the phone in my pocket and carefully slid the panel back in place.

Heavy banging at the door. Men with guns stood outside now. Boots kicked at the door, and the wood warped inward. It splintered in a thundering crash. The door to the lounge hurtled inward. I froze. My hand pressed against the sliding panel. It remained open a foot. Clunky black boots. A young male voice said, "No one here." An American accent. Not foreigners. What? I'd heard "Allahu Akbar," right? The lights flipped on.

"Check the closet," a different male voice said, sounding more like one of my students than a terrorist. "The window. Is anyone out by the cars?" he asked. I shut my eyes. The shelving pressed against the knots in my stomach.

Boots pounded the floor. "No one's in the parking lot," said the second voice, a little nasal and high pitched. "What you got?"

I squinted. There were big bulky black boots, and my eyes traveled up to tanned hands and in them a machine gun. The rest of the shooter was too high for me to see from my position. If I moved my head, I might see more, but fear kept me from trying. He'd spoken English well.

Two sets of boots. All they had to do was shove open the panel door and drag me out by the hair. They'd shoot me. I imagined my heartbeat so loud that it reverberated through the wood. Thinking of Edgar Allan Poe's horror story The Tell-Tale Heart, which we'd read weeks ago in class, I feared it would give me away.

A scream sounded in the hallway, and the murderers' boots spun around. I ducked to see a student just beyond the doorframe. I recognized Alice. She'd been in my class when I'd done my student teaching the year before. Go back, go back, I could yell. Distract them. The vibration of the gun split the air, and Alice's arms flailed. Her "I love Pink" T-shirt shredded to a red rag as blood spread over it.

She fell back out of my sight. A loud gasp escaped my lips. "God, no." The bottom of one of Alice's Vans tennis shoes faced me.

"What was that?" a voice asked. They'd heard me. As I shrunk into the shelves, the glitter in my hand hit the shelving. One set of boots turned toward me. Oh God, I'm dead. The boot stepped closer.

More screams came from the hallway. The boots pivoted. They were going after the kids. I could maneuver my fingers to grasp the jar. I should bust out of the tight confinement and throw the glass. Get the killers to come after me. But my hands wouldn't work.

I squeezed my eyes shut again, and when I opened them the boots were gone. They'd left. They would kill someone else, and I didn't do anything. I'd saved myself. I was such a coward. I began to shake.

Where were the cops? More gunshots. And then over a bullhorn–"This is the LAPD. You're surrounded. Put down your weapons, and let's end this peacefully."

There was nothing peaceful about that screaming and gunplay. But I took a deep breath. Maybe I'd get out of this alive. More gunshots rang out. I put down my head. Please let this end. Please come and save me.

After what felt like forever, I heard the patter of boots. "Shit, they got this kid right in the doorway." A voice close to me said. I squinted out to see black pants kneel where Alice's shoe had been.

Another voice yelled, "All clear. Is anyone in here?"

Before I could answer, the first cop stood. "No one's here."

"No." My voice was all air. I coughed and yelled, "I'm in here." I clawed at the paneling and wriggled out of the tightly pressed shelving, fearing I'd be trapped with gunmen unless I joined the police. They couldn't leave me. I pushed out the panel and tried to stand. My legs were putty.

I staggered and nearly pitched face first toward the floor. Squinting through the light, I saw the figures of two tall, clean-shaven cops with black vests blocking the door. Blue and red lights from outdoors washed over the wall, and black scuff marks lined the floor. That was where they had stood. Then my eyes traveled to Alice, and I shuddered as I averted my gaze.

"Miss, are you okay?" One brown-haired cop grabbed my arm. My tingling legs were asleep, and my head throbbed. But relief flooded me. I began to sob. A nightmare—nothing more.

The ebony-skinned cop placed a blanket over my shoulders, and I noticed the day had darkened. I stumbled slightly, and the officer caught me. I clung to him. My hammering chest tapped against his thick bulletproof vest an SOS in Morse code. He waited, his vest dripping from my monsoon of tears and my body sagging, trying to evaporate into the black protective vest.

It was like walking through a dream. The air felt dense and hazy, as if smoke blocked my eyes. My feet seemed to float across the tile where streaks of blood washed over the hallway from ceiling to floor. Sheets draped lumps that had to be dead kids. Numbness enveloped me. No, it isn't true. This didn't happen. How could it? I had to get out. I stumbled down the concrete steps of the front of the school and passed the bullet-riddled plaster sign displaying "Monroe High School." I almost asked why anyone would shoot up our sign before I realized how stupid that question was.

Bulbs flashed in my face. Click, click. I raised my elbow to shield my eyes. Reporters pressed in, asking, "What happened in there? How did you get away? Can you tell us how many are dead?"

The ebony-skinned cop on my right put a hand up as if to make a path toward the pulsating red lights of an ambulance. I pulled back. "No, I'm okay. I didn't get shot." His grip tightened on my forearm as I reared back and craned my neck to find my Prius. The parking lot was a sea of police cars and SWAT team members intermingled with cops, firefighters, and reporters. "I have to get my papers off my desk. I need to grade them tonight. Then I'll just go home. I only have a headache. I'm okay."

I started to turn to head back into the building to go to my classroom when my vision blurred. My knees buckled. Something soft and strong braced my head. I collapsed, and everything went black.

THE INTERROGATION

The light shone bright and hot, and my vision swam. "She's coming to," someone said, and I turned my head toward the voice. A nurse wearing blue scrubs grabbed my hand and pressed her cool fingers to the inside of my wrist.

Outside my curtained area, the sound of soft spongy shoes under hospital booties crept down the center of the open bay, and the beeping of monitors and a nurse being paged to the OR drifted through the gauzy white curtain that encircled me.

"Hi," the nurse said. "You doing okay?"

I nodded.

"I'm just going to start an IV. Won't feel a thing." She slid a needle into the soft flesh in the crook of my arm. I followed the needle to the tubing and up to an IV bag containing 500 milliliters of clear liquid. She smiled at me and turned. Her soft rubbery shoes made a shushing sound as they retreated through the curtain, which she pulled back with a metal shuffle of the curtain rings so I could barely see the curtained-off section opposite me in the large bay.

Someone coughed, and two people whispered.

And I remembered the attack. I sat up fast, and my head throbbed. The monitor next to my bed registered the P waves on my EKG rising and falling like a lie detector test. Dehydrated; get some saline in the patient, nurse.

An image of a man shriveled and burnt, thin, lying on a white sheet came to mind. He had bandages over his eyes, and the chart hanging innocently off the white railing of his bed at the Craig Joint Hospital in Bagram, Afghanistan, listed his birthday as January 1, 1980. It was an invented day as we didn't know when he'd come into the world, only that we were not supposed to let him leave it under our care. I shuddered and blinked once, twice, and then more to clear my vision.

No, I needed to leave the hospital. Too many ghosts of a past life. As I swung my feet over the bed, I noticed they were bare. Where were my shoes?

Suddenly the curtains were yanked back, their rings playing flat metallic notes on the bar they hung from.

Two men in suits entered with a uniformed police officer.

"Hello." The tall, sandy-haired man stepped forward, his smile as bright as the lights. "Ms. or Mrs. Fisher?"

I whispered, "It's... " I coughed. "It's Ms. Karen Fisher."

He jotted something down in his notebook.

I continued my search on the white tile floor for my shoes.

"I'm Dr. Swanson, and this behind me"—he moved aside to reveal a shorter, heavy man whose collar seemed to be strangling him, making his face red and giving him a pained look—"is Mr. Bradberry."

Mr. Bradberry gave me a two-finger salute and a feigned smile.

"Doctor? I'm okay. I just need my shoes." I dug my hand into the pocket of my black slacks and came up empty. "And have you seen my cell phone? It was in my pocket."

"I'm sorry, I'm not a medical doctor. We work for Homeland Security."

I located one of my low-heeled pumps peeking out of a white hospital bag by a chair crammed under the monitor and stood to retrieve it.

"We need to ask you a few questions," Swanson continued.

"About what?" I looked at the IV needle. I just needed to find a tissue and remove the needle, put a little pressure on the puncture, and get out of there.

"Where are you going?" Mr. Bradberry asked with a gruff, nasal New York accent.

As I started to slip the needle out, Mr. Swanson stopped me. "Don't do that. We'll only take a moment of your time, and then you can ask the nurse to remove that."

I stopped to study his face.

"We know the school was shot up. But what did you see?"

"I... I didn't see much. I was in the staff lounge when I heard it."

"What did you hear?"

I looked from Swanson's friendly smile to Bradberry's scowl. What did they want from me?

Bradberry sighed as if he were a bull in the ring with hot air snorting from his flaring nostrils staring down the matador and his rcd capc.

"I heard yelling, screaming, and gunshots. I think I heard the words 'Allahu Akbar.' And I called 9-1-1."

"'Allahu Akbar.' Was the voice foreign?"

"I thought so at first, but when they came in the room, they sounded American."

Bradberry took a step toward me. "So you did see them," he said in his nasal voice. "They came into the room."

"Well, not much of them."

"Not much of them?" The impatience in his tone was palpable. Swanson put up his hand and Bradberry turned away wiping perspiration from his brow.

Swanson's smile looked plastic. "Good, very good. You didn't see much of them, but you heard them. The voices: what did you hear, how did they sound?"

"Young. Like students. I need to find my phone." I looked at the metal tray. There was a plastic cup of water sitting on it, and suddenly I felt thirsty. I reached out a trembling hand and took a tentative sip. Cool on my tongue. Then I gulped it.

"We have your phone. Routine. We needed to check it," Swanson said. I glared up at him. Check it for what?

Bradberry, who was pacing, stopped and stepped forward. "On the 9-1-1 call you said 'I'm sorry. I can't stop it. They're killing kids. I can't stop it.' What did you mean, 'I am sorry, I can't stop it'?"

I tried to stand, and Dr. Swanson touched my arm. "Please just sit back. We will get you home soon."

"Where is my phone? I have to call home."

Dr. Swanson looked at Bradberry. Bradberry produced a plastic bag with my phone. He handed it to me.

As I slipped it from the bag I noted the black fingerprint powder on it.

Dr. Swanson continued standing so close to me I couldn't get off the bed without pushing him out of the way.

"Were they students?" he asked.

"I don't think so. I only saw their boots and arms and the assault rifles."

"But they didn't shoot you?" Bradberry studied my face.

Of course they didn't. I'm right here. "No, I told you, I was hiding. Wait—can't you tell if they are students or not? Haven't you questioned them?"

Swanson slid Bradberry a glance and Bradberry gave an almost unperceivable nod.

"What?" I asked, but my questions went unanswered as the men stared at me blankly. No, no. I jerked my head from right to left, trying to see a fellow teacher or student through the gauzy curtain. There were beds all around me in the bay. Someone else had to be near me. "Where is everyone else? You should ask them, because they must have seen more than I did."

Bradberry shook his head. His thin lips pressed together.

"What about Mr. Mackee's class? Did they get out?"

I'd seen bodies on the school floor, but no one had walked out with me. There were plenty of other exits from the school, right? Outside I'd only seen reporters. Shut up. I wasn't the only one with a hiding place. And there were windows in every classroom. The others must have opened the windows and escaped.

The men stayed tight-lipped. I started to shake and couldn't stop.

Swanson cleared his throat. "We have six students in critical condition and those who escaped through the parking lot. A few got out a window, but that's it. No one else made it. They were organized and took out the whole school in a matter of minutes. We're surprised you survived."

I pictured Alice again. The bullets riddled her body so her pink shirt turned to crimson. I could have done something. I could have distracted them. Tears spilled down my cheeks unheeded. My hands were so cold. I rubbed them together and couldn't stop. Suddenly I was cold all over.

Swanson said something else, or at least his lips moved, but if anything came out it was lost behind the whimpers that erupted from my throat as if a demon had possessed me. The last thing I'd said to James was that one day I hoped he would sit still—not knowing he might never move again.

The nurse reappeared; she tugged at my IV and bent to offer me some water, but I couldn't drink. She turned to argue with the men, who retreated. She smiled down at me, but then her face began to fade. Images swam in front of my eyes and closed to blackness.

THE QUESTIONING

I woke with a jolt, gulping air. The room had darkened, and I peered toward the window curtains. Dusk no longer tried to force its way through. Instead, the night's moon peered through the slit.

Then my eyes lit on the guard in the chair. Slumped over his face mashed into his closed fist. I sat up and his chin slid off his knuckles. He straightened. "Are you awake?" he asked. Before I could answer, he rose. He stood and pushed out through the curtained wall to my left.

Maybe five minutes later the suits came back in, and the lights flipped on. "We just have a few questions," the shorter suit, the one introduced earlier as Bradberry, said. "Then the docs can discharge you and you can go home."

I rubbed my eyes. "I just want to go home." But what would I do at home? And suddenly I wondered: had anyone told my boyfriend Steven where I was, or my mom in San Diego? "Where's my phone? I need to call people. Tell them where I am." I was still wearing the clothes I'd put on that morning before leaving for school. But my purse was locked in my desk at school. They'd given me my phone, but they must have taken it back.

"Don't worry," Bradberry said in his nasal, New York tone. "We let people know you're here and safe. We just need to finish this report." He took out a notebook that was identical to the one his taller counterpart had. Bradberry took the lead. "Did you ever see the shooters before?"

I shook my head. "Who are you again?"

"We're with Homeland Security. We told you. Now, did you see any workmen around the school or maybe phone lines that needed repairing?" he prompted.

Homeland Security. In charge of terrorist attacks. What did he ask? Oh yes. "No. I know the maintenance people at our school."

"It's just that they must have known how the school was laid out, to have been so thorough," Dr. Swanson said

"Or they could have had an inside person."Bradberry nodded towards Swanson. "Possible. Can you describe them?" He twisted his lips. "How many were there?"

I shrugged. "I... I only saw two. No, not saw them. Heard them and saw their boots."

"How did you get away from them?"

I glared up at him. Was that an accusation? Suddenly it dawned on me. I was uninjured, and they thought it might be an inside job. "I don't know them." What was I supposed to do, put myself in harm's way to save the rest? Maybe I shouldn't have survived. Swallowing the lump in my throat, I said, "I saw two sets of boots. Heard two voices. They spoke English well, but I heard the words 'Allahu Akbar' several times. Did anyone in Mr. Mackee's class make it?"

"You say they said 'Allahu Akbar' and spoke English good." Swanson moved forward while they both ignored my question.

I wanted to blurt out, "I said spoke English well," but thought better of it. "Yes." I answered down at my hands. "They sounded young. Did anyone survive in Mr. Mackee's class?"

"We're not sure. We'll check that out for you," Swanson said. "They sounded young, like disgruntled students?"

"Can't you tell if they're students?" I glared at them. "Didn't you ask for IDs? Are you questioning them?"

Bradberry looked at his equally clueless partner. "They didn't make it."

Home

The phone rang, jarring me from underneath the fluffy flowered comforter that had been my sanctuary for the last thirty-six hours. The previous day, Steven had told me yellow crime tape still circled the school building, and he'd refused to take me by it. "Reporters are camped out around the house," he complained. He did, however, pick up my purse from the police station. My cell phone was returned to me the night before. It still had fingerprint dust, and my numbers had most likely been copied and checked to see if either of the shooters' names was on it.

The ringing continued. "Steven, can you get that?" I asked, but when I peeked out from the comforter, I saw only eggshell-colored walls with the black and white photographs Steven had taken in Africa and Southeast Asia.

He must have gone to work. He still had a workplace to report to. The phone continued to ring. My head swiveled toward the carved wooden end table on my side of the bed, and I snatched up the phone.

"Hello." My voice was coated with pill-induced sleep. I coughed to clear my throat.

"Good morning," a too-chipper voice answered. "Ms. Fisher, this is Gloria Spencer at the LA Times. I wondered if you'd like to comment on the events that transpired at the high school."

Events? That's what shooting up a school is called? I guess I paused too long, because she started talking again. "You are being dubbed a hero for surviving the attack. What do you have to say to that?"

I scratched my head. "A hero." No, a coward. I pictured Alice again and began to cry.

"Ms. Fisher, are you there?"

I swallowed the strangling sob in my throat and said, "No."

My chest heaved uncontrollably, and it felt like Gloria's muffled "Ms. Fisher, Ms. Fisher" were miles away. When my breathing steadied, I threw the phone back down.

That night when Steven came home, he brought Chinese takeout, and I sat up in bed to watch the news. ISIS attacks in Syria and Iran had intensified. More innocent people died. Terrorists and terror everywhere. "And topping our local news. Monroe High—" Steven pressed a button on the remote, making the flat-screen, which spread over the front bedroom wall, go black.

"No, I want to see the news about the school," I snapped at him and then, embarrassed, soften my tone. "Please. I want to see it."

He looked at me for what felt like a full minute before pressing the button again, and the image of Alice filled the screen. A strangled scream started in my throat as the images scrolled past. And then my picture. The commentator's voice streamed in, "Student teacher Karen Fisher is one of the sole survivors. Twenty-four-year-old, Fisher was in Afghanistan for Operation Enduring Freedom and discharged from the Navy early." What did my being in Afghanistan have to do with anything? The words "inside job" flitted through my mind.

Next, the screen filled with the image of a bearded gunman. "Turn it up," I yelled. Steven glared at me before he complied. "Muhammed Khan, formerly Rodney Jasper, was an inmate at Lerdo Prison in Bakersfield, California, where he apparently joined the terrorist group ISIS. After being discharged from Lerdo, Jasper traveled to Syria, where it is believed he trained with ISIS for a year before returning to the US to plan this and many other attacks."

ISIS again. Terrorist again. When would it end? We were supposed to be safe from them, but now our own people were joining terrorist groups. I wasn't safe. We weren't safe. My phone made another shrill ring. I had turned it off for much of the day, but when Steven had returned home panicked at not being able to reach me, I'd turned it back on. There had been fifty-two missed calls, which I ignored. But, forgetting, I answered the current call.

"Ms. Karen Fisher, please," said a male voice I didn't recognize.

"This is she. Or her. This is me," I said.

Steven shifted on the bed so his face was in front of me and he mouthed the word, "Who?"

I shrugged the question off.

"Ms. Fisher, this is Mark Elliot from Channel Three News, and we would like to have a reporter meet with you at your earliest convenience."

"About what?" I drew out the words.

"We'd like your story about what happened."

"I... I don't know. Who is this again?"

At that Steven snatched the cell from my hand. "Who is this?" he demanded. Then after a beat, "She has no comment."

He stared at my phone. "There are eighteen voicemails on this, Karen."

I merely nodded. From that point on he took over my phone. "I'll get you another one so I can call you," he said.

That night, unable to sleep, I roamed the house. I shuddered at the shadows in my living room.

The red light of my laptop made me stop. Rodney Jasper was a member of ISIS—a word that seemed so distant a month ago. They had attacked my school. Who were they? I traced my finger over the wooden table in the breakfast nook and sat down in front of the computer.

I typed the word "ISIS" into a search engine. Dozens of results popped up for me to visit. Wikipedia reported that the Iraqi leader of ISIS, Abu Bakr al Baghdadi, had transformed scattered terror cells that had been at the verge of extinction into the most dangerous militant group in the world. "The aim of ISIS is to create an Islamic State across Sunni areas of Iraq and in Syria." Sunni? They wanted a country just for their own twisted fundamental beliefs in Sharia law. What did Alice have to do with their religious fight? She was innocent. They were all innocent.

My hand shook as I got a bottle of wine from the refrigerator. I had let them die and had done nothing. The computer pulled me back. I needed to know if there was anything I could find out about ISIS that could stop them. Or at least show me what I should do, could do. Whether something could be done. Did I sound crazy? I didn't know. Maybe I was. I couldn't sleep anyway. Every article claimed ISIS was well funded, very organized, and brutal. And they wanted revenge for Osama bin Laden's death in May 2011. I closed my eyes and pinched the bridge of my nose. When would the revenge end? How many would die?

I scanned article after article. Hundreds killed—British Aid worker David Haines beheaded. Villages captured—homes burned—Afghan police officers' families beheaded. And from my memory, an image of Alice and blood assaulted my thoughts.

And then, unbidden, another memory of the insurgent in my hospital in Bagram, Afghanistan. I had tried so hard to forget him lying in that hospital bed. He was all burnt flesh and bones hooked up to an IV. Yes, we'd tried to save him, but what had he done? Had he burnt a village to the ground with children? Had we saved him to send him out to kill more?

Suddenly I pictured myself. My hands bound. My neck exposed. I shuddered as I involuntarily pressed my opened palm to my throat. Just an image; that was all. I'd ignored the YouTube videos of the beheadings of reporters. But maybe they should behead me. I was guilty. Guilty of not saving them.

I paced the kitchen, frantic to find something to stop my mind. Steven had left a bag from the grocery store on the counter. I opened it. A razor. Not big enough to take off my head, but maybe I could slit my wrists. Stop. Oh, God. Stop it all. I dropped the bag and backed away from it. No. No, I'd survived. First Operation Enduring Freedom and now this ISIS attack. I was like the Ancient Mariner in that old Coleridge poem, cursed to walk this earth unable to die but also unable to tell my story so that it burned in my chest and the deaths of the innocent hung around my neck like the cursed albatross.

There had to be something I could do. Were there more like Rodney Jasper? Could they be all around us? I hadn't carried a weapon in Afghanistan, but I could get one and blow them all away. I wouldn't sleep until those bastards were all dead.

A bump sounded, and I started imagining shadows shifting in the living room. My glass of wine was empty, and I needed more to steady my nerves. Before I knew it, the dawn seeped through the curtains, and I slipped back into bed.

The third day following the shooting, Steven decided to drive me to the district office. There I'd fill out paperwork giving me an extended absence for mental anguish. The workman's compensation doctor would have to clear me to return to work . Did I even have a place to work anymore?

But before we even got to the car, I opened the door to the house and froze. Two white news vans and clustered groups of reporters stood in front of the house. Steven stepped in front of me. "Come on. Let's just get in the car."

Voices spoke from all directions. "There she is—the hero."... "How does it feel to be called a hero?"... "How did you escape?"... "Did you know the attackers?"... "Why did they let you go free?"

I pulled away from Steven and inspected the throng pressing closer. Steven yelled, "Get off my lawn, vultures."

I put up a shaky hand as a mic was shoved into my face. "What would you say to the parents of those students who died?"

Tears filled my eyes. I pushed back against the memory of Alice. Bullets riddled her body as she jerked back—while I stayed safely put. "I'm sorry," I croaked. "So sorry."

"Sorry? Could you have prevented this?" a voice asked.

Steven stepped in front of me and pulled me behind him. He shoved through the crowd. They closed in, pressing behind me. With downcast eyes, I hardly heard the buzzing of more questions flying around me like gnats at a picnic.

It was all over the news—my apology, speculation about my involvement, and more questions from the police. That night, unable to sleep, I slipped out of bed to go to my desk. The fat manila envelope lay on the desk: my things from work. I spilled out the contents.

First came the picture of me and my student council members. I traced the faces. Evelyn Yang, going to Berkley next year. No, not anymore. Someone else would take her spot, never knowing she'd died in the hospital four hours after the attack. My heart felt so tight in my chest, I couldn't take it. The sleeping pills hadn't worked.

I rummaged through the kitchen cabinet and found some of Steven's pain pills, 800 milligrams of ibuprofen. I took one. Anything to make the heartache go away. As if I were Lot's wife, drawn toward the destruction of Sodom, knowing the cost but unable to stop myself, I was drawn back to the papers on my desk. The essay that Jessica wrote about the symbolism in the Scarlet Letter. My comment in red, "More effort needed. You didn't cite the text with crucial evidence to prove the parallelism between the scarlet letter and the bloody letter 'A' carved in Dimmesdale's chest." I balled up the paper and hurled it. Who cared about the parallelism? Jessica was gone. I imagined for a moment carving a letter "C" for coward in my chest. But cowards aren't that brave. Instead, I shuddered as tears streamed down my face and then went to find the wine, too weak to bear Alice's screams flooding my mind.

At three a.m., my television options were limited. I stopped on an old 1977 spy movie called Telefon with Charles Bronson as an American agent trying to stop dormant KGB plants who were activated by a line from my favorite poem by Robert Frost, "Stopping by Woods on a Snowy Evening." A rogue Russian called the plants and said, "Miles to go before I sleep," and the plants became hypnotized to blow something up. Suddenly, I jumped up, overturning the bottle of wine I was sipping from because I'd run out of clean glasses. That's it. That has to be it.

Stumbling to the bedroom, I ignored the pain in my toe after stubbing it on the floorboard. I had to tell Steven. Leaning over the bed, I found his shoulder and shook him out of sleep. "I know what's going on. They're hyp-notizing prisoners at that prison in Lerdo. The one where Rodney Jasper came from." It was hard to concentrate, and my face felt rubbery. When Steven flipped on the lamp, the light hurt my eyes. "We have to stop it."

Instead of reaching for the phone as I hoped, Steven grabbed his glasses from the bedside table and squinted up at me. "Karen, what the heck? Are you dreaming? Did you have another nightmare?"

I shook my head. "No, no, no." My nose felt numb, and I couldn't feel my lips. I rubbed them to make sure they hadn't fallen off.

Steven didn't understand. He kept patting my arm and asking me to go back to sleep.

"It wasn't a nightmare. It's real." I finally gave up on him and went into the living room to find the number to Lerdo Prison. They needed to be warned. But I must have fallen asleep on the recliner in the living room because I forgot to make the call.

The next morning, I had to attend a mandatory session with a psychiatrist. Sitting outside the office lit with soft yellow light, I thumbed through the six months of People magazines with more leisure than I had waiting in the checkout line at Ralphs. I consulted my watch twice as the minutes ticked by. The brass plate with the name Dr. Le Carre centered the highly polished wooden door. Dr. Le Carre's secretary had been cheerful when I made the appointment, but there was no check-in or receptionist, just forest green cloth chairs and honey-colored wooden tables. Did she remember I had an appointment?

The door swung open, and a man in his early forties appeared, wearing polished shoes and a suit. He exited straightening his tie and without making eye contact. I pretended not to notice my fellow mentally broken patient as he dashed for the door to leave.

A young woman with hair that had reminded me of Alice's, strawberry blond, stood in the doorframe. "Karen? Karen Fisher?" Her voice was smooth like caramel. She extended a small soft hand. "I'm Dr. Le Carre, but you can call me Maggie."

How old was this doctor? Surely not old enough to have gone to medical school for eight years and do about a million hours of training before becoming a psychiatrist?

I followed her. Her black pumps whispered over the shag lawn carpet into the cave-like room. I headed for a blood-red couch. The lamp on the end table emitted a faint glow. How many scars had she opened up to pour that much blood into the couch? Sitting, I hugged one of the throw pillows into my lap.

She sat across from me in the matching red easy chair, a wooden table like a fire pit between us. On it sat a floral box of tissues with a white tissue extended like a flag of surrender. Had the last patient needed those? Because I wasn't going to cry, no way. Not in front of this stranger.

Meggie or Maggie lifted a notebook and pen off the table and smiled at me with the pen poised. "Okay, so what do you want to talk about?"

"How old are you?" I asked.

Her thin smile hardly masked annoyance. "I'm twenty-eight. Don't worry. I am fully certified." She pointed at the wooden frames holding papers verifying that she was indeed a doctor, not simply playing one in the soap opera that was my life.

She was four years older than me, but certainly I looked older. Well, to be honest, some of my students' parents had probably thought I was too young to safeguard their children's minds, and in the end I was too cowardly to safeguard their lives. What had she asked? Oh, right, what did I want to talk about? Nothing, actually, but thanks for asking. Instead, I said, "I just want to go back to work. There's really nothing to say."

The low lights reminded me of Girl Scout summer camp around the campfire when the troop leader told us scary stories of a murderer with a hook for a hand who roamed the forest killing innocent girls. Then one night, a couple in a car kissing and listening to the radio heard a scratch, scratch, scratch on their roof. Suddenly our troop leader had yelled "Boo!" and we'd all screamed and laughed and slept with one eye open all night.

But this time I was supposed to tell the tale of killers storming a school and Mr. John Mackee scratching on the cabinet where I hid, saying, "What the hell, Karen?" Scratch, scratch. "What the hell?" My students screaming as the corpses were thrown in the campfire, their blood pouring over this couch, keeping it bright red. The psychiatrist, one of the girls, shrieking, and boo, they're all dead. Except me, because I have to stay up all night with one eye open.

"Maybe we can start with what happened that day." She looked over the notebook with her emerald-colored eyes. Expecting me to say... what?

"That day," like she knew any day like that day. I noticed one of my fingernails was uneven. Using my teeth to straighten it, I spat the nail carcass so it bounced on the table.

The psychiatrist took the tissue and grimacing picked up the spat nail. I took a deep breath. I had to say something to get her to prescribe some antianxiety pills so I could close my eyes and not see John Mackee scratching—scratch, scratch. In the end, I spilled their blood to save myself again.

Maggie or Meggie or whoever broke eye contact after my summary of the event and looked at her notes. "And how did that make you feel?"

Was she for real? Terrific. How do you think I feel? I shrugged instead. "I'm here. I guess I should be grateful."

"But you're not?" The sculptured eyebrows lifted.

What was she, some kind of genius? "Of course I am. Why wouldn't I be? I survived." I was one of the only ones who crawled through the dirt to see the campfire again. "I'm here. Hallelujah. Thanks be to God." Now give me some pills to help me close my eyes and not see the blood they spilt.

THE AFTERMATH

My head throbbed as Steven patted the comforter. "Why don't you invite some of your book club friends over? You need to see people. Get back into things."

When I didn't answer, he said, "Janet called six times and Kathy called again last night. I told her to call you and set up a time to stop by. Also, Alexie and Veronica from aerobics called to ask when you were coming back. Karen, you can't just ignore your friends. You have to call them back or you're going to end up all alone."

I had listened to the calls from Janet and Alexie asking if they could come see me. Veronica had rung my doorbell unannounced and entered with a basket of muffins and margarita mix. After ten minutes, I'd told her I had a headache instead of suffering more of her sympathetic looks and her Southern belle chorus of, "You were so brave."

Steven's look demanded an answer.

"I called my mom." I had done so about a dozen times.

At first she was concerned. "Oh, honey," she'd said. "We were all so worried when we heard the newscast. Should I come down there to help you? You didn't look so well when those reporters photographed you at your house. Did you forget to wear makeup?"

But when I'd called her accidentally at two a.m. the next night, she seemed more impatient than anything else. "Karen, have you been drinking?"

"What does that have to do with anything, Mom? Every time I close my eyes I see them."

"What did the counselor say?"

"That counselor doesn't know anything."

"Well, if you have that attitude, of course the counseling won't help. Did you tell her about the dreams?"

"Yes."

"Well, don't get angry with me. It's the middle of the night, and you woke up your stepfather."

I'd pushed the end call button with as much force as I could. The next morning, she called to say she was sorry she'd been so short with me. "But really, Karen, how do you expect to have any friends if you speak so fast and so angrily?"

Angrily? I almost screamed at her, but I was so tired all I wanted to do was get off the phone.

Steven's voice brought me back to the bedroom. "I can't keep making excuses. Call them."

I stumbled into the shower at 11 a.m. and went to get just one more glass of wine to stop my headache and found the cupboard bare. Then the shrill ring of the phone in my hand almost made me jump. Instinctively, I looked at the number. The keypad read, "Kathy."

I eased the green phone icon down. "Hello?"

"Hello, stranger," her jarringly cheerful voice replied. "I've been calling you all week. I'm just dying to see you. I saw all those reporters on the lawn. Steven told me you might be up for a visit."

"There's no food in the house and I don't have any wine," I said.

"No worries, dear. I'll just pop by the wine cellar for some wine, crackers, and cheese. How about an assortment of lunch meat as well? We'll have a little party, dear."

What? To celebrate the deaths of everyone else at my school? What a grand idea. We could even invite the reporters to get the whole thing on tape.

As if reading my mind, she asked, "Are the reporters still all over your lawn?"

"I don't know."

"Can you look and see?" she asked.

I tiptoed to the curtain in the living room as if the reporters might hear me in the house. After knocking my knee into the hulking wooden coffee table and dodging the burgundy easy chair, I inched open the thick fabric of the curtain. Two news vans were parked across the street. A female reporter with a pixie haircut had cornered my neighbor, who pointed toward my house as if she'd seen me. I immediately dropped the curtain.

"Still there," I said.

"Okay." Was it my imagination, or did she sound pleased?

Forty minutes later, Kathy sat across from me in the easy chair. She'd just had her dark hair streaked with blond highlights and wore a flowered dress that looked a little chilly for the overcast morning. "I swear," she said breathlessly, pouring me some wine in a plastic cup because all my glasses were dirty, "those reporters are persistent. They cornered me for fifteen minutes asking all about how I knew you and if the police had questioned me about you."

Questioned her about me? "What did you say?" I asked.

"I told them we were best friends." She reached over the heavy wooden coffee table to where I perched on the love seat and handed me a cup of red wine.

I swigged from the cup as her French-manicured nails fiddled with the curtain and her eyes scanned the front of my house. Then she patted her hair down and looked back at me, leaving the curtain just a few inches open. I held my cup out to her, as she still held the wine bottle. Her brown eyes widened. "Oh my. Some more already? Here." She poured the wine and put the bottle down between us. She plucked a Ritz cracker and slice of salami from their cellophane wrapper and plopped them on her tongue before settling back against the fluffy head rest of the easy chair. "So what was it like?"

I shrugged. What was it like watching Alice's chest explode and feeling paralyzed? What was it like closing my eyes each night just to be visited by Mr. John Mackee's pleading expression, "What the hell, Karen? What the hell?" and not having an answer. What was it like having not only the media flock my house but so-called friends too? The same friends who constantly canceled dinner plans with us were suddenly acting as if a UFO had landed in my living room and they had to get a glimpse. I stayed quiet.

The phone rang again, and I moved away from the coffee table where it sat. Kathy plucked it up. "Blocked call," she announced.

"Don't answer it. It's probably a reporter," I warned.

Smiling, Kathy pressed the button and held it to her ear. "Hello. Kathy Johnson. Karen Fisher's BFF," she said. And I wanted to snatch it back. Who said "BFF" anyway? Teen aged girls. What a phony. The resentment I'd felt a dozen times when Kathy came to book club without reading the book and insisted on making tons of comments anyway flooded me. Why was she in my home?

"Well, Mark Elliot from Channel Three, we'd be delighted to do an interview with you. Next week? We'll pencil it in our PDA. No problem." She winked at me. "We'll be there."

"Pencil it in our PDA," what did that even mean? What bullshit. I wasn't going to any stupid interview. I grabbed the wine bottle, poured some more, chugged it and ignored Kathy's surprised expression .

HITTING ROCK BOTTOM

"The whole room smells like a drunk tank," Steven yelled through the blankets piled high on top of me. He yanked them down. "You need to get up. Take a shower. You need help, Karen. You can't keep drinking like this."

I grabbed the pillow to ward off the assault on my eyes. My head ached. "Didn't drink that much." I heard my muffled and slurred words through the cotton. My head pounded. Did I have any more of that red wine left from last night? Red wasn't my favorite, but I'd polished off the white the night before. It had helped, too. I hadn't seen Alice's or James's faces in a few days.

I felt Steven's weight plop down on the bed, making it droop precariously. A clash of imaginary cymbals crashed against my temples, and I swallowed acrid bile that hit my throat as if I were seasick. "Karen, you've got to stop this," he said. "What does the counselor say?"

I didn't answer.

The warmth of his hand seeped through the comforter to my leg. "This can't go on, Karen. I know you were there, and you saw that student get shot."

I lifted my pillow. "Alice. Her name was Alice." I slurred because my mouth felt numb, like I'd just been given novocaine at the dentist. Why'd he have to open the curtain anyway? I closed my eyes and replaced the pillow.

"I don't know what to do for you. I poured out the booze, but you sent your friend out to buy more." Yesterday, Veronica had returned with wine, and later that day a woman I hardly knew had visited, pushing through the reporters. Their only requirement for entrance was a bottle of wine, but I accepted whiskey and brandy in a pinch. "And now the sleeping pills are gone. You can't just lie here the rest of your life."

I thanked God he would have to go off to work in fifteen minutes. That afternoon I must have dozed off, because I woke to the low murmur of the television and the sunlight peeking through the curtains in the living room. My neck was stiff from holding it in an odd angle against the cushions of the love seat.

I don't know how long I had been asleep, but I woke from a gunman chasing me in an all-too-familiar nightmare. With a raging headache, I squinted toward the kitchen. My heart started at the figure hunched over the sink until I recognized Steven bent over the faucet. He made a little sniffling noise, and I stood up to see what had happened. He must not have heard me, because he didn't turn. "You're not at work?"

He jerked upright, turned, and wiped at tears behind the lens of his glasses. "It's five." His voice was nasal, a sure sign he'd been crying.

"What's wrong?" I asked.

Then I noticed he held the framed black and white photo he'd taken via tripod on Maui the summer before. "Steven, is something wrong?" Had some else died? Maybe another school had been attacked.

He put the picture next to the sink, which was full of wine glasses that needed washing. When he didn't answer, I asked, "Did you cut yourself?"

He shook his head. "Karen, we can't go on like this."

"Like what?" I asked, getting a little angry he'd be upset about a few dirty glasses when I had lost all my students in a single day.

"You have to do something besides crying, drinking, and wandering the house all night." He came over to me and put his arm on my shoulder.

I shrugged it off. "It's only been a week . I saw those gunmen, Steven. They killed Alice right in front of me. And you're mad about a few dirty glasses?"

"It's not the glasses." His beautiful blue eyes were red behind their glass barrier. "You need to let it go. Get help. And it's been more than a week—it's been almost three weeks . This needs to stop."

"I lost my students, Steven. My friends. I'm not going to just get over it. You have no idea how that feels."

He dropped his hands. "Yes, I do. The Karen I know didn't survive that attack either. She's gone, and no one understands that. They all say how glad I should be that you survived, but you're gone. You aren't the person I know and love. And I don't know how to get you back." He looked down and his chest heaved as his eyes spilt more grief on his cheeks.

I could have hugged him close and promised him everything would be okay. But I wasn't convinced it would be. My head hurt, and I felt I'd get sick if I didn't get some coffee. I knew I should reach out to him, but I couldn't...

I just couldn't. How could I comfort him when I lived the nightmare like an endless movie clip?

I sat in front of the television as Steven packed a few bags. Some stupid soap opera was on the set. A girl was bawling because her boyfriend's twin had survived and assumed her boyfriend's identity or some shit. I only turned around when Steven stopped beside the love seat, dropped the extra set of keys and a note on the coffee table. "I'll call you in a few days. Maybe we just need a break, but I can't watch you self-destruct. I'll come pick up the rest of my stuff in a week or so unless you decide different." He looked down at me, and I could see he'd been crying some more. I could have asked him to stay, promised him I'd change, but maybe he was right. Maybe the girl he once loved had died when those gunmen entered my school. She certainly deserved to.

At the door Steven whispered, "I love you." Then he was gone.

*   *   *

Kathy came over to help me dress for a television interview, she'd insisted I undergo "to set the record straight." Whatever that meant. I considered backing out, and because my hands were shaking, she poured me a brandy. The stuff burned going down, but I drank it and another glass for courage before we drove off.

There were bright lights and people handing me bottled water. Someone messed with my hair. Katie disappeared to circulate and talk to news people. Another girl took my arm to help me on to the stage, but I flinched because she looked like a student. Was I dreaming? The air seemed to warp. I clutched the girl's hand and she looked frightened. "Sorry. I'm so sorry." I squeezed her hand, wanting her to understand that I didn't mean for her or any of them to die that day. She acted like I was speaking French.

Things were a bit swimmy, as if the whole thing was happening under water. My stomach hurt, and the man who sat in front of me smiled too much. Why was he so happy? Behind him, the screen filled with pictures of the kids. He said something, but I didn't understand. One image after another flashed by. So young. Why them? I had trouble forming words, and I couldn't remember what the guy with the too-perfect teeth wanted me to say. Then I didn't want to be there anymore, so I got up.

Two girls in blue T-shirts and ponytails materialized as I almost tumbled down the stairs off the stage away from too many questions. I bumped my way down a white-walled corridor and out at the red exit sign. Some white-haired man, wearing glasses that flashed in the lights of the underground garage, helped me find the car .

*   *   *

The vehicle's wheels wouldn't work, and I blinked, trying to focus. Red and blue lights washed over the car. I jumped at the rap on the driver's side window. A dark figure loomed through the glass. The car door swung outward, and I gripped the steering wheel. The man asked, "You okay?"

"Yes. Car stopped working."

"Must be that tree crumpled into the front end."

I scratched my head. "Oh." What could I do?

"Have you been drinking?"

"No. I... I'm just going home. Leave me alone." I tugged at the door.

"I'm going to have to ask you to get out." The door wouldn't close, and he grasped my arm and pulled. No, I just wanted to go home, so I flung my arm out to stop him. He must have been angry because he slammed me hard against the top of my car. My head hurt, and he flashed a bright light in my eyes.

WHERE AM I?

My nose itched, and through my clogged ears I heard the buzzing of fluorescent bulbs somewhere. I blinked and looked up. Ouch; everything hurt. I felt the pressure of a cold, hard floor under me. I squinted to see the thick bars on the cell and noticed my mouth was open and my tongue rested against the concrete pressing into my cheek. I straightened up. "What the—?"

On the bench a man sat, leaning his elbows on his knees. He had on the same type of black boots that the killers had worn. I squinted up at the blond hair on his forearms and his broad chest. Not my house. Not Steven. Was he a cop? Not a uniform. I scanned the words "Dept. G" in white letters plastered on his black T-shirt, which stretched over defined pectoral muscles. Department G? What the heck? Above his chest his muscles were so thick he had practically no neck, and his lips formed a straight line. His tanned face sported a slash mark scar like he'd been on the wrong end of a knife fight. And his expression changed to a smirk.

He could beat me senseless with those fists. I scooted back and hit something. Stopping, I drew my knees to my chest. I shook. What did he want? He stared wordlessly. He looked like a commando in some television show.

I swiped a hand across my forehead. I didn't see a gun, so he wasn't going to shoot me. "Who? Where... where am I?"

"This is Department G." He didn't sound angry.

"What... ? Why am I here?"

"You were brought."

"Brought? By whom?"

"Department G."

"What? That's not an answer." I swallowed the vomit burning an acid hole in my throat.

His lips twitched. He found this funny?

"Who are you, some kind of guard?" I was caged, so it must be some sort of prison. I started to stand and realized one of my flats was missing. "Who stole my shoe?"

He shook his head. His hair was cut short to the scalp, and a few scars showed white against the skin under the hair. His eyes were brown with green flecks.

He rose and pushed the buttons on the DVD player bolted to a black metal shelf hanging from the ceiling.

A close-up of my face filled the screen. The black eyeliner around my blood-shot eyes streaked down my cheeks like a Goth chick's experiment. I was on the television? The picture zoomed out so that I saw my dress, the one I still wore. Oh, the interview from the night before.

On the screen, I leaned forward in a chair across from the interviewer. "No," I slurred. "They're everywhere. Terrorists. We're not safe. We'll never be safe." I bobbed my head like some crazy person. The newscaster's eyes bulged as though he'd swallowed a golf ball as he handed me a box of tissues. I hit the box away, and it bounced on the stage.

I'd seen enough. My head throbbed. Why was the crew-cut stranger showing me this? Why not save it for the criminal trial I was pretty sure I'd be looking forward to in the near future, if my bits of memory from the night before were correct? "Turn it off," I yelled, but he ignored me.

Back on the screen, the forty-something reporter brushed back a few strands of hair that had managed to escape his hair spray. "But you survived." He gave me his toothy smile. "You made it out. You're being called a hero."

On the screen, I'd stood up, tottering on my feet. I stepped out of one of my shoes. Okay, one mystery solved. "They died!" I yelled. "They all died. I hid, okay?" More tears streamed down my face, which was inches from the interviewer's. "I hid and they all died." Spittle flew from my mouth, making the interviewer move back. "What could I do?" I pulled back and shook my head, more tears falling. "I didn't do anything." My eyes squinted, and I looked confused or constipated.

"I gotta go, okay?" I pivoted right and then left as if lost. Then I must have spotted the steps because I turned. The screen filled with my rear end. I staggered to the rear of the interview stage. The camera caught the two young women I remembered from the night before. I held on to the shoulders of their navy-blue Channel 3 T-shirts. They helped me down the steps, and I disappeared. The camera went back to the interviewer, who shrugged and looked wide-eyed into it. Kathy pushed her way on to the stage.

The screen became a patchwork of black and white squares. I glanced at Mr. Crew-cut, who unfolded his extra-large biceps and pushed a button so the screen became black. "You ready to stop whining and get to work?"

He left without my answer. Work? Before I could contemplate it, I stumbled over the metal toilet that pushed against the back wall. Sinking to my knees, I heaved the contents of my stomach into the bowl's open mouth. I was sick over and over until my throat burned and stomach ached.

I slid down on the floor too weak to move. I don't know how long I sat there before Alice's and James's faces filled my mind. I heard heavy footfalls and opened one eye from where my head rested on the floor. A metal tray of food was pushed through the bottom bars of my cage, and I struggled into a sitting position to see the departing figure of a medium-sized person dressed in black jeans and black T-shirt. I climbed to my feet and unsteadily rushed the bars. "Hey. Hey, wait. What do you want from me? You can't just keep me locked up."

The figure and the sound of his feet disappeared, and I sank to my knees. "I need my sleeping pills." Tears slipped down my cheeks against my will. "What do you want?" I whispered. "I need my medicine. I can't do this."

I avoided eating in favor of pacing. The thought of food made my stomach flip over. My head still hurt. Calling for help beyond the prison was out. My purse and cell phone were missing.

They couldn't just keep me locked up. "I have rights." Rushing the bars, I grasped them as if I could shake them loose. "You can't just keep me locked up. What do you want from me? What do you want?" I wasted more energy attempting to bend the bars. Then I stopped. A noise. There was someone else around. Someone moving below me?

The cell sat on the second floor. In the center, it opened to the first floor. The prison block had metal railing wrapped around the ledge as far as I could see. It had identical rows of cells on each floor. Above me were two more floors topped off with a flat ceiling with the same urine-colored paint job.

"I know you can hear me." My knuckles turned white wrapping around the bars. "Answer me. Damn it! Answer me." I let out more frustration on the bars and screamed. "I need an attorney! How about my phone call? You took my cell phone. People will miss me. I'm a hero. I'll be missed. Don't you know who I am?" When I stopped, sweat dripped from my cotton dress, and my throat was raw.

The sun had gone down by the time my stomach growled, and I ate the cold eggs and bacon from one of the two trays by the front of my cell. The bacon tasted greasy, so I went for the peanut butter sandwich on the second tray that had materialized sometime after I'd paced the cell so long I'd finally fallen onto the mattress and dozed off.

After eating, I rocked back and forth on the mattress. My throat was still sore from screaming in the silent cell and throwing up. I'd go crazy. Maybe they'd just kill me. I laughed at that. Not a laugh of humor but of the insane. I didn't die in the shooting, but they'd kill me in the stinking cell like a cowardly rat. Then it would finally stop. I laughed again. The hero would die hidden in this trap.

Department G

The artificial light was the only indication of day versus night, so I guessed it was lunch on the second day when the plastic-wrapped sandwich and apple laden tray slid into my room delivered by the still unspeaking jailer. "Thanks, Harry," I said to his nameless back. He didn't turn around and introduce himself. "How's the family doing?" I called through the bars. No response from the figure disappearing from my sight. "Oh no, don't worry about me. I'm grand. Going to the high school prom tonight in the same dress I've worn for two days now... What's that, you say? Now that you mention it, I could use some help with the television. Damn thing's busted."

During the night, I paced and wished for something to help me sleep or, in desperation, for the ability to turn on the television and watch anything. I'd gotten on my tiptoes and jumped, but it was up too high for me to reach.

I plunked down on the cot and tore away the plastic wrap. As I sank my teeth into a second bite of tuna and celery, the screen blinked to life. Mr. Crew-cut, who I hadn't seen since the day before, appeared on the grainy TV screen, his bulky arms crossed. Behind him a vast background of desert and sand dunes materialized.

"By now you are probably wondering what you are doing at Department G," he said.

"Well, duh, Frank." I'd given him a name, too.

"Each of you was chosen because you have a military background." As he paused, I wondered what my being in the Navy had to do with my imprisonment.

I'd gotten out in 2013, two years before. I left directly after my deployment to Afghanistan for Operation Enduring Freedom, where I was with the 415

Expedition Wing doing medevac missions. A spark of alarm hit me; one reporter had asked me whether my military training had helped me survive the school shooting. Was it a coincidence? If it was, Department G would be disappointed, because my deployment hadn't taught me to fight or helped me evade capture. No, I survived the school shooting because I was hiding in my rat hole.

As a medic, in the Navy, I'd tried to save lives, but when someone was getting shot at, I was pretty useless. My war experience had been eight long months in a shoe-box-sized B hut with four other junior-grade lieutenants at night and in the hospital during the day.

My host, Frank, continued, "And each of you has a personal reason to join our fight against terrorism." He had said it again—"each of you." So there were others. Where? I swiveled my head to look out of my cell. I thought of that noise I'd heard the day before. I rose and went to the bars to scan every room I could see. Over three dozen cells, I estimated. There didn't appear to be life in any other cell.

I turned back to the screen as Frank kept talking. "ISIS is not going away. The terrorist organization is growing and spreading throughout Syria and Iraq. It has infiltrated our country and other nations." The screen flashed to a man dressed completely in black from hooded head to toe. He carried a large sword and stood over a kneeling figure. "Steven Sotloff's killer, a British SAS member."

I bit my lip. And then there was Muhammed Khan, formerly Rodney Jasper, who shot up our school and whose name I'd never forget. I turned my head away. I didn't want to hear what the video had to say. I didn't need any reminder of that day of death. On the screen, Frank said, "It's time to fight back. You've been picked to help with that fight." I peeked through my fingers as static filled the screen before it went black.

So that was it. I was chosen because Frank and whoever else thought I was a hero too. Hadn't they shown me the awful video? Were they too stupid to realize I was no hero?

That night I dreamed of Alice, James, and Jessica kneeling before a man dressed in black. His face was covered, and he lifted a big sword. I screamed as he brought the sword down and cut the heads off the students. Alice's and Jessica's heads flew at me, and James's rolled under my feet. Blood splattered over my face. I couldn't breathe. Bolting upright, I sat on my mattress. Just a dream. Just a dream. My hands shook, and I needed a drink badly.

Then my heart jumped to my throat as I saw the shadow cast inside my cell. My heart wouldn't stop racing until I noticed it didn't move and I made out a stack of... what? Towels? Clothes? I walked to the stack. Two pairs of gray sweats and white cotton underwear. I'd worn the same dress for two and a half days. I rifled through, finding a pair of white socks with tennis shoes, size eight, my size. And there was a canteen. I shook it. Full. I put it to my lips hoping for wine. But water splashed over my lips and dripped down my chin. Where was Jesus when I needed his wine-making technique?

There was also a towel, a bowl of water, and shampoo. I yearned to wash off the scum. The lukewarm soapy water felt good on the black soles of my feet. After washing away two days of alcohol and fear-laden sweat from my arms and legs, I dressed in the clean, warm sweats. They looked like the ones the Army soldiers wore. Somehow I fell asleep without more dreams for the night.

I woke when the doors to my cell clanged open. Climbing to my feet, I looked at the television set and waited for some instruction that didn't come. Swiveling my head from side to side, I expected something. Someone to jump out and yell at me. Stupid. I'd wanted nothing more than to escape, and now that the doors were opened, I was paralyzed.

A loudspeaker announced, "Everyone report to the first floor for PT." I hadn't heard the term "PT" since the Navy. It stood for physical training. Not that I'd been inactive since I got out of the Navy. No, I had yoga on Saturdays, or at least I used to before that day. And then my Tuesday night aerobics class. So I stayed semi-active. And besides, that was about all I could fit in with all the essays and tests I had to grade. I'd also toyed with the idea of one day writing the great American novel that would move people to tears. My fellow book club members had all joked that we needed a scandal or tragedy to push us into the spotlight. Funny what happens when you get what you wish for. But no, I never had managed to get a word down on paper.

On the ground floor under me, I saw a group of nine people dressed in identical gray sweats. Frank emerged clasping a clipboard. I examined my fellow prisoners. They were of varying shades, heights, and body types. A set of stairs descended to the first floor at the end of either side of the row of cells. The steps to my right were closer, but I'd have to go by Frank. So I pivoted and marched to the other side.

When I got to the bottom floor, Mr. Crew-cut made what looked like a check on a list. "Form up," Frank said.

"Excuse me." I wedged my way between a plump woman with blond curls and a leathery-skinned white man. The woman slid to her left without a word, and the man stood immobile, glaring. I figured I couldn't look as ill-fitted to be there as they did. Everyone fashioned straight lines at arm's length from each other. I followed suit. What are we getting in shape for?

Frank yelled out a series of commands like, "Assume the position," and I got into a push-up position like everyone else. I must have something in common with these people. I didn't have time to look for that something—anything—that I must have in common with these strangers, because Frank called, "Give me twenty." The rough floor dug into my palms as I tried to move my arms up and down with a burn that reminded me that I'd lost the strength to do what I could two years before. Staring out the corner of my eye, relief washed over me as I realized I wasn't the only weak one.

The sweaty, chubby woman cried out and fell flat on the ground as Frank crouched, his face inches from hers. He taunted her like a drill sergeant. "Get up. What's wrong with you?"

I survived through a series of ordered jumping jacks, knee bends, and sit-ups. As I swiped sweat from my eyes, I looked around at the muscled guys who stood directly in front of me. They looked built for a mission of kicking terrorist butt. When would Frank realize he'd made a huge mistake with me?

He barked another command: "Now follow me as we double time it to the track for a run." No one looked me in the eye. Speculation on the curious disparity among these strangers nagged at me. Had any of the others survived a terrorist attack like the video claimed? Did they wrap their cars around a tree while too drunk to realize they hadn't just run out of gas?

The African American woman to my left looked like she lifted weights and moonlighted at a biker's bar nights after long days of kicking puppies. A tall, nerdy, bucktoothed guy still wore his military-issue eyeglasses—the kind called birth-control glasses because allegedly no one would sleep with the wearer. I thought he'd have trouble getting a date without them. Next to him walked the leathery guy who looked too old to kick any terrorist butt. Not that I was qualified, but this guy's smoker's cough made him sound like he was born with a cigarette clamped between his teeth.

What the heck was I thinking, checking everyone out to see if they were more or less qualified to be saviors of this world? Like I could even do it. Like Department G had any right to kidnap people or to make me their Nikita, their trained assassin. No, I had people who would protest my disappearance and try to find me. Unless…

What if they faked my death? By the time this occurred to me, I'd walked outside the large metal doors and was squinting out at an oval shaped dirt track with a grassy middle. It was hemmed in by gray buildings on every side. A slate sky with a few cumulus clouds hung over us, which made my throat constrict. Nothing more. No hint of where I was. Was I still in Los Angeles? I had to be. Wouldn't I remember a flight or a trip to somewhere else? That's assuming I could remember much.

Frank yelled, "Pick it up! Come on, double time." For some reason I looked behind me to make sure I wasn't the last person. No, not last, but almost. Only the short, chubby push-up failure looked bug-eyed scared behind me. I moved faster to distance myself from her.

After the first lap, I felt winded, and my unused muscles screamed at me. I rushed to the side of the track and almost threw up. My hands shook, and I wished I had some of that brandy Kathy had brought by the house. As I looked up and met Frank's glare, I started running again. I finished all four laps. Toward the back of the pack but not last. Frank's shouts made my throat ache with memory. After what I assumed was a mile run, Frank yelled, "Fall out for the showers and chow." But I wasn't sure I wanted to play anymore. I wanted some answers, and not just his cursory explanation that our world was going to hell. I wasn't in the Navy anymore. No, I wanted to hear my charges, plead my case, and make a decision myself. I wanted to know what I'd been drafted for.

I went back to the cell to get my dress. I'd wear it despite the vomit that still clung to the sleeve. I'd give them back their sweats and make for the door.

After chugging water, I grabbed a towel and turned to hang it on the bars to shield the other cells from my room so I could dress. But before I could thread it through the bars, Frank stepped into my room.

"You going to the showers now? 'Cause after chow we have an appointment to talk about your future."

"No," I said. "I'm leaving." I shook the towel. "This is for some privacy when I change back into my civilian clothes." Then I felt stupid for explaining myself to the Neanderthal.

As I went toward the door, he grabbed my arm. "We need to talk."

I reeled around to face him and snatched my arm back. "No, we still live in a country where I can make my own decisions."

He crossed his arms. "Have you seen yourself?"

I hesitated. "What business is that of yours or Department G? If I want to drink wine and sleep all day. What business is it of yours?'

"Waste," he said as if words were expensive.

"My life. My waste. I don't even know who you are."

"Doesn't have to be."

"What do you know about it? I'm not a terrorist hunter. I'm a teacher." His blank face infuriated me. "What are you, crazy?"

"We know."

"You know what?" I jutted out my chin as a challenge. "That I'm not up for this? What is this?" He looked at me with his dumb blank expression. I wanted to punch him. I should just leave. But for some reason I stayed rooted in the same spot. Curiosity or just that I have nothing else? I didn't know but I wanted to. Maybe he could make the dreams end. Maybe he had the recipe. "Did you kidnap me? Where am I? What do you want?"

I noticed I was close to his face now, yelling. He smiled, so I lashed out, smashing him in his stupid dimpled chin. He grabbed my arm and twisted me so I was pinned against the wall facing him. "Are you going to try that again?"

I dropped the towel and looked out of the cell bars, wondering suddenly if we had an audience. But no one was visible. Not one person would come to my rescue if this caveman wanted to kill me. The heat of his hand warmed my wrists. He was so close I could feel the warmth of his breath on my face. "What do you want? You can't make me a killer." My eyes traveled to his mouth as if to read words there but realized too late it looked like one of those cheesy movies where the actress looked down expecting...

As if it were a signal, he leaned in and covered my mouth with his. I didn't want to kiss him. Why should I, with all the unanswered questions and the matter of my kidnapping? But closing my eyes as if hungry, I tasted his lips, and my tongue probed between his teeth. Heat rose, spreading from between my thighs to my lower stomach. It took all my strength to push back, breaking the spell. I had trouble forcing my eyes open. I couldn't catch my breath. His pine aftershave made me dizzy, and I wanted to kiss him again. Get lost in that kiss. Instead I bit my lip and took two shuddering breaths.

DO I STAY OR DO I GO?

"Go. If you want, you can go." He let go of my arms. Then he stepped aside.

"Why? What's this about?" Suddenly I didn't want to leave anymore. I didn't want to decide what to do. I wanted to be told.

"I've been where you are. We need you. We can help."

I wanted to ask him about the kiss. What did it mean? I yearned to know him. But what if that was just a ploy? Heat rose into my face. I felt ashamed. I'd cheated on Steven with a stranger. And what if it was just a way to get me to work for them? I whispered, "I'll stay for now." I didn't look back as he slipped from the cell.

Frank didn't speak to me again until the next day. I'd been asked by a new jailer to sweep and mop the kitchen floor and wipe down tables. The plump push-up failure had disappeared, and to my surprise, so had the two muscular guys I felt sure were perfect candidates for terrorist butt kicking and the man who seemed minutes away from emphysema.

Six of us were left, and the large cafeteria with its two dozen metal prison-looking tables seemed like a scene right out of "The Walking Dead," a show I hadn't been able to stomach since that day. Which in some ways felt fitting since Department G seemed to think the apocalypse was days away.

None of us talked. There were a few times I wanted to approach the others, find out their stories, see if they knew where we were. But everyone ate with their mouths close to their metal mess trays and with eyes cast downward. To be honest, I didn't know what to ask, and asking meant I'd have to tell my story, and I didn't want to. Instead, I tried to imagine what they'd been through and why they were there.

Frank said he'd been through what I had. I wanted to know that story, and I intended to ask. In fact, I intended to get answers from that word-deficient hulk without another day passing. And that was when he stopped by the entrance of the cafeteria and in predictable fashion said one word, "Fisher."

Like the obedient dog I'd become, I jumped up. I had to remind myself not to run after this man who had kissed me just to get me to go along with the physical training and manual labor. I wasn't even sure why he wanted me here.

I passed through the double metal doors and proceeded not toward the track we had visited every morning but to an area I hadn't seen yet. It was a prohibited area where Frank and the other five jailers I'd seen sporadically that week disappeared when they weren't ordering us around. One had demonstrated the way to disassemble various machine guns the day before. Another had demonstrated how to use a radio and refreshed our memories on the military alphabet for messages—which I didn't see how I'd use because I wasn't carrying a gun or a radio.

Beyond the doors ran a corridor with three doors on either side. Frank continued to the last door on the left and pushed it open. He went in, not waiting for me but holding the door open until I entered. It fell shut with a sucking sound as I entered the darkened room. It was designed entirely of metal and hard right angles. What did this room say about the man who sat in it?

I eased down into the black and chrome chair in front of the dented metal desk that might have been a throw-away from the ancient office of a non-commissioned officer. Frank leaned forward with steepled fingers. A clipboard lay atop the desk.

"So?" I asked to avoid squirming in my seat or trying to picture the curve of his lips or that little scar that traveled down it. "Now what?"

He smiled and leaned back. "So. Here's the point where you decide to stay or leave. This is where you make a commitment or you go back to drink yourself to death."

"You don't know the first thing about me. That video was a fluke," I lied. "I had too much to drink one time and you think you know me?" I felt my face contract as if my words were bitter. "I went through something, okay?" The lazy droop of his eyelids conveyed that he was not convinced by my words.

"I saw my student get shot to death." And as that seemed too little, I added, "Right in front of me. I knew her. She was a student of mine. Do you hear me?" My breaths came quicker, and I felt that telltale sinus pressure and heat in my eyes that came right before a crying fit which I was not going to have, not in front of Frank.

I broke eye contact and stared at my shaking hands. After I blinked several times, I looked up at him. "You said you knew what I went through. What did you go through?"

He nodded and crossed his arms, but though I stared at his lips, they didn't move.

"You know what happened to me." I moved in my chair. "And all these people. You said we all had an experience with terrorists, but I don't know anything about what they've gone through. And I don't know why you need us. What does this have to do with ISIS? What's your story? Why do you want to keep us in the dark?"

He didn't move anything but his lips when he said, "So do you want to stay and work, or do you want to piss the experience away?"

"No." I stood up and leaned over the desk. "No more questions. I want answers. Or I'll walk out that door"—I pointed at the door—"and not come back. And another thing, where are the others? Did you kill the lady who had trouble with push-ups or the guy who could hardly breathe?"

That got a brief chortle from Frank. "They left. Walked out the door. And you were always able to do the same."

"I don't even know where I am."

"The real question is, why are you still here?" he asked.

"Maybe I'm just curious. Maybe I want to know… to figure out what to do." Now tears slipped past my eyes onto my cheeks, but I tried to swipe them away with fingers that weren't as absorbent as tissue. "Maybe I'm tired of seeing the faces of dead kids and I'm wondering if you have an answer. Do you have an answer? Because all I'm getting is more questions. What are the answers? Because if you don't have any, then I'm gone."

"Sit down," he ordered.

"Don't tell me to sit. I'll stand unless you have nothing. Then I'll go anywhere but here, where you promise something you don't deliver."

"I was on Seal Team Six." He picked up a metal paperweight, the only other item besides the clipboard on his desk. "We went after Osama bin Laden." He flipped the metal object over in his hand. "Headlines reported a helicopter crash. In Afghanistan. Twenty-two dead. But not all. I know what it is to be the only one left."

I swallowed the lump in my throat and slumped down in the hard chair. "But you didn't hide. You didn't let them die and do nothing."

"No." He leaned his wrists on the desk again. "I ran. Disappeared so everyone thought I died in that crash too. And maybe I did."

I let the silence linger a while, until I felt I'd bust, before I asked, "And then what?"

"I heard them screaming every night. I wondered if it would ever end. The terrorism. I drank to silence it." His Adam's apple bobbed as he swallowed. "Then I got a chance to do something about it."

"What?"

"We started Department G. Our mission: stop terrorism."

"How?"

He flipped the clipboard around so it faced me. "First, you have to enlist with us."

I leaned away from him. So he wanted me to blindly sign something without knowing what I was getting myself into. I'd done that before. Corpsman. GI Bill for school. All those dreams of working in a clean, safe hospital. All the illusions of comforting the sick. And I'd gone where I got to see people crippled by IEDs and burned beyond recognition. True, I didn't know them, but years later when I closed my eyes, I could still see that Afghan man, an insurgent, in the bed—all bones, burns, and blind eyes.

When I got home, my mother wondered why my dream had changed to teaching English. How could I tell her of the horrors I saw? How could anyone understand I'd just had enough? "Why did you choose me or that woman who couldn't do push-ups or that man who could hardly breathe, and what happened to those two tall, muscular guys who looked like they were ready for combat?"

"Told you. You all have military or law enforcement background and a reason to help."

"Law enforcement?" Suddenly it hit me. "That cop who pulled me over. He was one of you? Whoever you are?"

"Yep."

"And that woman, who couldn't do a push-up, why was she here?'

He sighed loudly enough for it to be intentional, a signal of his impatience. So what if I bothered him? I'd been patiently playing along with this Department G for days. I deserved answers. I repeated, "The woman, the weak one, why her? Or the smoker? And where are the others?"

"Daycare worker, former Navy like you. An estranged parent came into the center. Held 'em hostage. Two kids died. She's not here anymore because she wanted to go back to overeating and sitting in front of the television. To forget."

I winced. "And the smoker?"

"Pentagon on 9/11. Security guard. A woman died in his arms. And before you ask again, he wants to be left alone to smoke and drink himself into the grave."

"And those other two who looked like terrorist hunters?"

"Cops. I asked 'em to leave."

"Wait, you want me, a teacher, a daycare worker, and a security guard but not cops who are trained to interrogate and shoot?"

"Department G isn't here to hunt down and kill every terrorist. That would never end."

"So why are you here?"

He leaned back, leaving the clipboard and my enlistment paper in front of me. "The salary is $1,500 during training, $2,000 plus room and board on the job. Not a fortune, but you're still pulling disability pay, right?"

"I don't know. Where does the rest of the world think I am?"

He flipped a few pages on the clipboard and slid a paper out and over to me. It took me a moment to realize it was a police subpoena for my computer. There was a list of all the ISIS sites I'd visited. "Oh my God. Are you saying that they think I'm part of this?"

"They're looking into it. You ARE one of the only survivors. And your cell phone records." He shoved another paper from the clipboard under my nose. "You called Lerdo Prison asking for anyone who knew Rodney Jasper."

I racked my brain. That night, I'd woken Steven and wanted answers about the prison. I didn't remember, but I must have called it. Had I been that out of it? I'd been drinking heavily. Was I in that much trouble? "So they're looking for me?"

"We've leaked a rumor that you're in Mexico in rehab, and it wasn't a hard sell. However, there are cops who still want to question you about your possible involvement. When you sign, you also agree no booze."

Asshole. "So I could say I don't want to join and I can just walk out these gates. No prison? No consequences?"

"And no protection. Your choice."

I thought about it. I could leave and be a suspect. They couldn't put me in prison, because I hadn't done anything. I thought about the Salem witch trials and The Crucible, the play we'd read in English 11, a satire on the McCarthy communism hearings of the 1950s. People became scapegoats all the time. Putting that aside, would I be able to go back to teaching? That was, if they ever released me from my diagnoses of post-traumatic stress disorder. But what would I really be going back to? Worry about the next attack. "How do you know I'm not involved?"

"Because I've been where you are. And it doesn't lead anywhere good. When they took away my gun... " He flipped me the insides of his wrists. Long scars traveled vertically up each.

How could he know how many times I'd thought about using Steven's razor or a pill overdose to end it all? I'd even tried but ended up with my head in the toilet. "What do you need me to do?"

"Nothing violent. Maybe even working with kids some of the time."

"Wait a minute. You're recruiting kids to fight terrorists?" I'd heard of child soldiers in Somalia, and I'd known of soldiers in Afghanistan who'd found bombs and guns on kids, but we were Americans, for God's sake.

He smiled. "No, we're training these kids so they never become terrorists."

"I don't get it. I wouldn't have to kill anyone, just do what I'm already trained to do?"

"No killing. On my life." He picked up the pen and handed it to me.

A morbid thought hit me. How much was his life worth? He'd tried to off himself. But so had I. When all those students and teachers had been killed wishing for life, we'd both tried to throw ours away.

I needed someone to tell me what to do. I needed someone who understood where I was coming from. I needed something to do to avenge the kids I'd lost. So with a shaking hand, I asked, "How long?"

"A year or as long as you like after you sign the nondisclosure."

"What are you going to do that I can't disclose?"

"We work underground so terrorists don't know how to stop us."

It didn't make any sense. But neither did an attack on unarmed teenagers. How was teaching kids fighting terror? He'd promised I didn't have to kill anyone. I was curious and I couldn't see myself going back just yet. "And my present job?"

He extracted more pages from his clipboard. "We have the paperwork for your leave of absence for a year or more. It's all handled."

My head shook as I put the pen to paper. I took a deep breath and scribbled my name. Before I turned to leave, I looked back at him. "One more thing."

He looked up from his papers. "What?"

"What's your name?"

That seemed to startle him, and his mouth opened and closed.

"You stuck your tongue down my throat but you can't tell me your name."

He sighed. "That was a mistake. A momentary lapse in judgment. Won't happen again." He straightened up the papers on his desk as if they had been in disarray to begin with. Then he spoke down to his lap. "Owen." He waited a beat before asking, "Is that all?" And then it was.

GATHERING INFORMATION

When I sat down to dinner, I moved closer to the five remaining terrorist fighters. The ebony-skinned athletic woman looked like she might beat me up if I asked her anything. Two benches in front of me sat two guys, facing me. They sat shoulder to shoulder but didn't speak. The younger one, maybe in his mid-twenties, had pale skin and jet-black hair. I guessed he was from East Asia. The other was possibly from India and maybe in his late thirties. I hesitated before I ruled out approaching them. A pair was one too many for me to start with.

 I glanced at the last set of benches, where the craggy-faced Middle-Eastern-looking man frowned down at his food. Okay, then, there was one, the bucktoothed nerd boy.

"Hi," I said and had to cough as my voice failed.

He looked up and stared at my mouth like he might have dreamt me speaking to him. "Hello," he said and shoveled a forkful of meatloaf into his mouth.

I extended my hand. "My name is Karen. And yours?"

He wiped his hand across the paper napkin. "George Harrison. I know what you're thinking—like the singer. I get that all the time, but I'm a chemist. Dealing with brain chemistry."

My breath caught. Brain chemistry? I thought of that movie Telefon, where fifty-one Americans become walking time bombs with a key sentence triggering the alarm. Could Department G be hypnotizing kids? Were they waiting for them to grow up like in the movie and become killers? Was I supposed to be their teacher? Oh God, no. Was I crazy? It wasn't possible, but I had to find out more.

As if a co-conspirator, I slid closer toward him, which caused his eyes behind those birth-control glasses to widen. I whispered, "Do you know why you're here?"

"I don't know how much I'm allowed to say. I read the fine print of the disclosure they gave me."

"I think that's for people outside Department G. But we're both inside."

He pushed his glasses up his nose. "Still, I better check."

I leaned back. "Never mind, I'm just curious because I'm a teacher." I wanted to kick myself for just jumping in like that. "Owen said we all had terrorism in common. My school was shot up. I'm one of the only survivors. What happened to you?"

"Owen?" He asked.

So this guy didn't know the mysterious crew-cut Seal Team Six member any more than I did.

"Yes, Mr. Crew-cut. He said on the video that we had all been touched by terrorism in some way."

George swallowed so deeply that his Adam's apple, which in his skinny neck looked like a dagger, cut down his throat and disappeared into his breastbone . "I... I was working with pharmaceuticals that a disgruntled employee used to poison some children's aspirin. Twelve kids died. There was a trial and investigation. I trusted him, you know. It caused nationwide panic." I remembered hearing about that on the news. It started somewhere in DC—not in California. If that was where we still were? "I went into the drug business to make a difference, not to kill innocent kids." I wondered if Department G wanted him for that purpose—to drug innocent kids. If so, he was about to have his eyes opened.

Looking across four tables, the African American woman's coal-colored eyes glared into mine. I waited for her to turn her back. She wore a sleeveless shirt that emphasized her biceps of steel. She wore her hair in multiple braids and a red bandanna across her forehead. I nodded my head toward her. "What do you think she does?"

"She's probably one of the trained terrorist killers," George said. He'd mirrored my own suspicions.

I looked around the room and motioned toward the two men sitting side by side forking food into their mouths. "And those two?"

"I heard one talk." George dabbed his nose with the paper napkin. "Said something about a bombing at an abortion clinic, and the other's a computer hacker responsible for disclosing the safe houses of at least six murderers in witness protection."

"Whoa, really?" Impressive group I was with. "You have been talking to the others?" I crossed my arms. Chemist, teacher, hacker, and killer. What did we all have in common? I thought of Walt Whitman's poem "I Hear America Singing." What would good ol' Walt think of our group with all its modern professions?

The metal door to the front of the cafeteria opened. I'd never seen outside the front of the building. Through the door, a black SUV sat, and a man in a suit walked in before the door closed again. He grabbed the lapel of his suit coat and smoothed down the collar.

Owen exited from the back offices and hustled toward the stranger. They both ducked into the front side offices—or what I imagined were offices, like the ones where Owen had escorted me. I wondered what was in the black briefcase the man carried.

No one appeared to be guarding the door, and the garbage can was only a few feet from it. I'd never been through those doors. Would the floor plan be the same? One corridor with offices on either side. If so, there was a lot of empty space between the back and front side doors.

Time to do some surveillance. As I rose to take my trash to the can and slip through the front side door, two more suits entered the front. I sat back down, my heart hammering rapidly against my ribcage. Okay, if I did this, I had to play it cool. Who, me? I was just looking for Owen to ask about my mission and future training. Didn't I have a right to know what I was supposed to be doing? It didn't say "keep out." Where was all the mutual trust anyway?

Finally gripping the tray to steady my shaking hands, I got up and went to the trash. A glance behind me told me only George was looking at me. So I smiled at him and dabbed at gravy that stuck to the metal of the tray. Now or not at all. I slid the tray into the soapy water beside the garbage and headed for the door.

With my head lowered, I turned the handle. Taking a deep breath, I slid in. No one yelled, "Hey, where are you going?" so I closed the door to my back and closed my eyes to thank God nobody stood in the hallway.

To my left were glass windows about eye level—not good for climbing out of. I ducked as I noticed the tops of men's heads sitting around a conference table. Most wore suits except Owen, still wearing his traditional black T-shirt with tight jeans. Two other men wore the type of loose pants and tunics I'd seen in movies with Middle-Eastern men. I ducked and crept toward the closed door.

I heard a deep voice say, "The airstrikes are continuing. But we don't like their lack of direction. Too many casualties of war. Our mission is more centralized. We have eyes on the ground. Smith is acting as a news reporter in Kobani, near the Turkish border. The town is taking on heavy artillery, but it's still holding. We have intel on our major bad actors. Kafferdy, what do we have with these new recruits? It looks like pretty slim pickings out there."

The suit must have been talking about us. Anger flashed through me as I thought of being judged like rotten grapefruit. Then again, I wasn't a brave terrorist hunter, so it kind of fit.

I saw flashes of light as if a slide show was going on. Because the light was playing over the far wall, I felt safe looking over the ledge and into the room. The fluorescent overhead lights had been dimmed, and the men sat facing a presentation. No one yelled, "Hey you, what the hell are you doing there?" so I felt safe. A photo of the African American woman in my group flashed across the screen.

She wore Marine dress blues, and the caption under the picture read "Lance Corporal Daisy Ross." Daisy Ross? She looked more like a Samurai Sue or Martial Arts Meg. "Dishonorable discharge due to civilian shootings in Iraq," Owen said. So he had to be Kafferdy. "She's spent the last three years bouncing at a strip joint called the Purple Pussy Cat."

Laughter rose and the first deep-voiced speaker said, "Excellent," as he shook his head.

Owen went on, "A few arrests for drunken brawls. But we scrubbed her record. She's good to go. New identity, CO for Lerdo Prison. New name, Latoya French. New cover, transferring from Las Vegas as no current CO has worked there."

"Wait a minute," a man wearing flowing clothes and speaking with a heavy accent said. "Why not put in a man? He could infiltrate Muhammed Johnny's recruits—maybe even get into Syria close to the others."

Kafferdy cleared his throat. "We're working on that from another angle, and it takes time. With shootings going on in LA, we need to take that bad actor out quickly. Ross is an African American, so Muhammed Johnny will be more likely to let his guard down, and she'll strike to make it look like an accident."

A picture of a bearded, turbaned man flashed on the screen. "He's heavily protected, but once we take him out, Lerdo won't be such a threat." Owen was talking about the prison Rodney Jasper came from. I accidentally scraped the window as I tried to get as close as I could to the picture of the guy who must be a religious leader.

I ducked as a head spun in my direction. A voice asked, "Is there someone out there?" A murmur sounded around the room. The voice added, "Go check."

AFTER THE KISS

Oh God, no. I couldn't run back to the mess hall as I didn't know who was on the other side. Even if I was stopped in the cafeteria, they'd catch me before I got to the stairs for sure.

I darted away from the mess, down the hall and around a corner. There were a few more doors on each side. I yanked the handle of one. Locked. My palm got slick with perspiration as I tried another. Then another. All locked. Shit. Hurry, hurry.

I sank against the wall and held my breath. I heard the conference door open, and my eyes lit on the white metal garbage can.

The lid was one of those swinging triangle-shaped ones. I could take it off and slip in, but who knew what trash it held? No choice. Fear trumped hygiene, and I snatched the lid off.

Peering into it, I saw paper and an ink cartridge but nothing else. If I crouched, I could fit. I stepped high and hopped to get my shaking leg in. Fear hammered in my chest. I couldn't afford to bump the metal and give myself away. I slipped my other leg in and hit the bottom with a thud. I froze, expecting to be besieged, but no one yelled.

I squatted. Replacing the lid, I cringed as it banged against the top in my trembling hand. Looking up from the darkened bottom of the can, I watched the lid wobble and the flap swing back and forth. My fingers wrapped around the lip before it crashed to the ground. I held my breath as I eased it into position. The flap swung faster.

Footsteps grew nearer as my heart hammered against my ribs. I heard a voice close. "No one out here. Wait… "

My head swam as I remembered being in the cabinet. My chest tightened as the memory of constricting shelving, squeezing, trapping me, flooded my panicking mind. I was blocked in while killers shot my students. I trembled, imagining Mr. John Mackee's face that last time, asking, "What the hell, Karen? You're leaving us to fight alone while you hide?"

Snap out of it. Think. I noticed the lid oscillating, and, holding my breath, I placed my finger on the edge. Footsteps outside the can made me shudder. I touched the paper next to my knee. I could shove it into his hand if he placed his fingers through the swaying flap. Shame enveloped me. When I had glitter jars in the cabinet, I didn't throw them to distract Alice's killers, but now with lower stakes I could finally act. It would serve me right if he snatched the lid off. He'd haul me out and drag me in front of the conference.

Did I care? Somehow, I did.

As I tugged down on the metal, something touched the garbage can. Then another voice said, "Check the mess. Then circle back." The shadow lifted from the can, and the footsteps retreated.

The plastic ink cartridge poked into my ankle, but I dared not move or else I'd crinkle the paper. I counted to one hundred fifty before I felt safe peering through the swinging flap.

My legs were lead. I tried to stand and banged the sides of the can unsteadily. After stepping out of the can, I slowly lowered the lid. I wanted to see what they had to say about me, but I'd have to wait until night when I could sneak in. I'd only seen the conference table, chairs, and a side table where a pitcher of water sat and a few plates of fruit. I didn't think they kept files in that room, but Owen Kafferdy had an office with a file cabinet. I needed to get a peek in his files.

The next day after PT and chow, we had classes on current events featuring ISIS propaganda videos. The videos showed cars and trucks blown up and citizens chased down at gunpoint and shot. I closed my eyes, pressed my lips together, and cried for my kids and all the others running but not getting away from ISIS. Following the videos, I was sent to do laundry and given three additional gray sweats.

After lunch, the rest of the trainees and I sat in a circle in the middle of the mess with the tables moved back against the walls and a mat on the floor. Owen stood in the center wearing a white martial arts getup.

"Today our self-defense class will deal with simple tactics." Daisy Ross—the name still made me laugh—raised her hand when Owen asked for volunteers. "Okay, Ross. You think you can take me on?" he asked, circling her with his fists raised, blocking his face and chest. She lunged at him, and he sidestepped her attack. He struck the back of her knee with the sole of his foot and took her down with an elbow.

She bounced back up and circled him. He waited until she swung before he sidestepped her again, and she landed face first on the mat. Her eyes narrowed as she jumped up ready to rush him. He flipped her over his head, and she lay blinking until he reached down to help her to her feet. He bowed to her. She frowned as she returned the gesture.

"Okay, you can take a seat," he said. "Fisher, you're next." Had I heard right? Daisy snorted through her nose as she sat.

"Who, me?" I pointed at the middle of my chest, and he nodded. I shook him off. "No, that's okay. Don't think I'll need it." Unless I was training kids to be killers.

"Fisher, you're up." He waved me over. So I stood.

"First come toward me and grab my wrist." He placed my hands on his wrists. I squeezed. With one jerk downward he released my grip, stepped around me, and with his leg against my thigh, shoved his elbow in my back making me fall forward. It knocked the wind out of me. I lay face down tasting rubber mat before I rolled onto my back.

He towered over me with his hand out to help me up. The urge to kick him in the testicles flitted through my mind, but why provoke a bully? I rolled my eyes and attempted to stand on my own, but he grasped my forearm and hauled me to my feet before I could protest.

That was it, he deserved to be hit. I raised my knee to his groin, but he sidestepped me. Another elbow to my back and my face once more bounced off mat. "You need to stay on your toes and be ready for any attack."

Screw him and his Department G. All a big stupid secret. When I rolled over this time, I aimed my foot to his shin and kicked with all my might. He bounced away and gave me a muted kick to the ribs. It hurt mildly, but I knew he could have caused internal bleeding if he'd wanted to. He was toying with me. I rolled around and got on all fours. Stars danced before my eyes, and I seethed. "Watch where the attacker's eyes go. Anticipate what she might do next."

I breathed out a shuddering breath. I bet he couldn't have anticipated those killers at my school. Did he think he could take them on with his bare hands? When he reached down to help me up, I grasped his hand and threw myself into him. He flipped over and together we plunged to the ground. He lay on top of me, his face inches away. His gaze burnt into mine. "Never let your guard down," he said to the others.

My breaths came heavy, and I felt my heart race. His warm exhalation was inches from my face. "You going keep fighting me?" he whispered.

Not thinking of the pain, I attempted to head butt him, but his hand stopped me by pinning my cheek to the mat. His head dipped. Lips tickled my ear. "That's good. That's the fire." And when his lips touched my skin, I tingled all over and wanted to kiss him. I wanted him to make love to me right there on that mat. It was sick, I know. For the first time since our last kiss, I felt alive.

FALLING FOR OWEN

It ended when he sprung to his feet and helped me to mine. I turned and walked back to my cell. Behind me George yelled, "Where you going?"

Owen said, "Let her go."

I kept the tears in check until I got to my bunk. There I buried my face into my pillow. I beat the pillow, imagining I was beating my weak self. Tears streamed down my cheeks unchecked. I hit the frustration at not being able to save them. I beat Rodney Jasper over and over again. Then I struck out at myself for letting this stranger make me feel alive when I had given up on Steven. I needed a drink. A drink would help me forget that I was a monster. I couldn't do anything right. Somehow I fell asleep.

It was dark when I opened my eyes and started at the figure standing at the door. And in that flash of a second, I realized I hadn't dreamt of Alice or James and that I was in Department G's prison, not home. Owen stepped into my cage with something wrapped in plastic in his outstretched hand.

"Dinner," he said as he tossed a sandwich at me. I grabbed it seconds before it collided with my nose. Without being invited to do so, Owen sat on my cot.

The heat radiating off his skin made me nervous. "What are your plans for me?" I picked at the plastic wrap, revealing the corner of a peanut butter sandwich.

Only one side of his lip lifted into a smirk. I couldn't stand it.

"I know that you're sending Ross into Lerdo to kill Muhammed Johnny. What do you have planned for me?" I jutted out my chin feeling tough.

He snorted. "I knew you were in the trash can. You have to learn to do it better if you plan to go into survcillancc."

"You come to insult me or give me information?"

"To make sure you don't starve."

I still clutched the sandwich, hungry but trying to avoid eating in front of him. "If I'm useless, I can't imagine I'd be any good to you or Department G."

"I didn't say you were useless. I said you had things to learn."

"Well, let me enlighten you. I froze when those killers came into the school. I could have distracted them, maybe given Alice a chance, but I couldn't do it." I turned away from him, not wanting him to see the water standing in my eyes.

He took my chin in his large palm and turned it to him. "You'd be stupid not to be afraid, but we aren't asking you to do anything you can't handle." In his eyes I thought I saw understanding, even compassion. We'd suffered alike. We lost the same amount. Maybe from that loss we could find something together.

The fire in his palm sent a shiver through me. "What are you asking me to do?" I asked again, and then I spotted the keys on the chain that held his dog tags against his chest. Our gazes locked as my pulse quickened. I leaned in and kissed him, wondering why he made me feel alive and want to be alive—something I hadn't felt in the last three weeks.

He returned my kiss and pushed me back on the mattress. The heaviness of his hips crushed me as his hands traveled down my chest and pushed up my gray sweatshirt. He shoved up my bra, and his mouth found my breast. His lips and teeth teased my nipples. He bit, and sharp pain shot through me. I clutched his shirt. Stretching it, I yanked it up. He sat up while I shoved the shirt over his head.

He fell back onto me, his chest pressing down on mine. His heart drummed against mine. His lips played close to my ear. He bit the lobe. A numbness lifted. I wanted to claw my way back. Back to life. Momentarily, guilt flooded me. Steven's lovemaking had been tender, not rushed. Owen's touch was hard, rough, all edges like the man. With his lips by my ear, he whispered, "Do you have protection?"

I took Owen's face in my hands. My hungry lips found his, pressing into them hard as if sucking his breath from him. This was really going to happen. Maybe Steven was right; I'd died that day. I wanted to live. I wanted someone to make me feel anything but that death, that fear, and that guilt at not acting.

When I released him, out of breath, I couldn't answer his question.

Instead, I shook my head. He leaned back. From his tight jeans, he took out the condom and extracted it from its foil. He unbuttoned and unzipped his pants. With one shove he pushed them to his ankles. I averted my eyes from his penis growing larger in his hand, and then he removed my sweatpants without a minute to spare.

My legs opened as he settled between them. My flesh felt on fire as his teeth raked across my neck. He thrust into me and set a rhythm—like he was pounding a nail. He rocked with a frenzy that made me hit my head on the wall, and I pushed up against it. His fingers pinched at my nipples and his teeth bit at my neck.

I invited his punishment. With each thrust and bite, I arched my back rocking with him, wanting to forget about the last three weeks and the blood and death. Then he tensed and released a low groan. He went still on top of me, his breathing rapid. Seconds later, he slipped out of me, and my heart thundered.

How I'd changed. Now, I was the girl who had one-night stands with men I didn't know. I was the girl who needed this strange man to feel again. I was the girl who threw away Steven, the man who gently massaged the skin above my hip bones. Steve who would search my face as if it was a book he could read while I waited, getting more excited. He'd ask if I was okay before slowly entering me. Steven, who loved me so much, he let me rock while his fingers softly massaged my breasts until I exploded. Only then had Steven taken his own pleasure. Steven loved me. Owen didn't. Could I make him? Why would he love a coward? I wanted him to. I wanted to matter.

Feeling dirty, I swallowed more guilt and fingered Owen's keys and dog tags. I could slip them over his neck and go to his office to find my file. As my fingers worked the chain over his head, he opened his eyes. I dropped the tags to the side of the mattress. His eyes bore into mine. "You okay?" he asked.

How to answer? My genitals burned but I nodded. Then he rose on all fours and turned me over with a powerful push. I wanted to feel him inside me again. I wanted to feel anything. He got behind me and thrust his stiff penis between my buttocks. He entered just as roughly, and I held on as he pitched back and forth, clasping my hips in a death grip. When he collapsed for a second time, his hands gripped me to him like a straitjacket. His mouth was next to mine, his breathing rapid. He buried his face in my hair. "God, I needed that. I haven't felt that alive in forever."

No "I love you." No soft caress. What had I expected? I struggled against his embrace to turn around and face him. "What do you mean?"

His cheek pressed against the pillow on the bed. He pushed away strands of my hair that had fallen into my face. "I needed you," he explained. "I got no one else. Not anymore."

My eyes stung with threatening tears. I was alone too. "Tell me," I said, wanting to know him, to love him. To make what we'd done special.

His lips buckled. "When our helo crashed, I lost my team. I got lost too. Someone took out my whole team, and they didn't know I was alive. No one got it. I was supposed to feel grateful, but my friends, my brothers were dead, and I was running for my life."

He was telling me more than he had all week. He continued, "I didn't want to survive, but I told you that." Instinctively, I found his wrists and traced the lines where a razor had once cut deep enough to drain his life.

He sucked in a breath. "God, I want you again."

My eyes watered and I placed my finger on his lips. "Then what? What did you do after the crash?"

"I lay low, not knowing what to do. Cheap wine, prostitutes, and fights. Then Department G helped me find a purpose. But I see you." His hand brushed my cheek. "I feel something in my gut." He averted his eyes. I swallowed a lump growing in my throat. "God, this can't happen. I'm your training officer. But you make me feel again." He looked at me. "You know?"

At his pain, my stomach fluttered. I barely knew this man but that didn't seem to matter. "I need you too," I whispered. I cupped the back of his head and kissed his lips. He returned the kiss and then settled back on the bed.

"I shouldn't stay. But I'm so tired," he said, his voice rough as if exhausted.

"Where do you usually sleep?" I asked.

"My office," he said.

I nodded. "Then stay. But I need you to touch me softly this time. Can you do that?"

"Was I too rough?"

"A little." I missed Steven's touch. Steven's love. But Steven was part of my old life, the one where kids didn't die. I took Owen's hand and put it between my thighs. Then I placed his other hand on my breast. "Soft," I told him and soon I too arched my back and exploded with pleasure.

His face examined mine and he smiled. In that smile my heart lurched. Maybe he did care. Maybe he could love me. The me I was now. Kissing my forehead, he rolled over, and his breath became slow and shallow. I inched to the edge of the bed. When I heard his snoring, my feet hit the cold floor.

THE BAIT

After washing him off my skin with the cold water from my canteen, I crawled under the bed and retrieved his keys. Just as my hands gripped them, my stomach growled. I froze, but the snores continued.

Damn, I had to take the sandwich with me. I slipped from my cage with a quick look at the muscular contours of Owen's back as I left.

On the first floor, the muted yellow lights at the sides of the doors barely lit the dark prison as I picked my way down the stairs. To my extreme relief, the doors weren't guarded. I walked to the door, closing off the mess from the set of offices that Owen had taken me down two days before. I tested the handle. Not locked.

The office hallway had no lights. I thought about propping the door open with a table or the trash can, because darkness meant terror and nightmares. Men like Owen always had flashlights. I wished I had checked his jeans, but I wasn't going to go back now. Okay, I had to man up and close the door. I eased it shut and pushed down my fear as I trailed my fingers over the doors, counting one and then two. I heard a creak and stopped, but nothing jumped out at me. I traveled on to the third door. I felt for the keyhole.

The keys dangled from Owen's chain, and I fit the smallest one in the lock first. Damn, no go. The third key worked. Easing the door open, I stopped to listen for any noise. Nothing, so I closed it and, taking a deep breath, stumbled over the carpet to the desk. I flipped on the lamp.

With my sight revived, I attacked the file cabinet using the small gold-colored key. Why was my hand shaking? It wasn't like I was breaking any laws. I slowly inched the drawer opened.

George's name was on the first file. Did I have time to look at what Department G had in store for George? I looked back at the door. How long would Owen sleep? What if he woke? Not finding me there, he'd come look.

He'd know what was up the moment he didn't feel the weight of his dog tags. No, I had to move on. I pushed the file down and mashed the one behind it.

I took the file out to straighten it up, but a page with a picture of the young Asian computer hacker fell out. Under it were pictures of guys who sported beards and long scraggly hair. What was that? I read the names Jihadi François, Jihadi Marcus, Jihadi Abdul, and Jihadi Alan, who had the striking green eyes of a European. Had any of them shot up schools or cut the heads off journalists and aid workers? Were these guys, born in countries besides Syria and Iran, so entranced with Sunni fundamentalism that they killed for it? What made a person do such a thing?

I read the information. There were family names and locations and something called weak links. They were in the computer hacker's folder, so his job must include all of them. I doubted he could take them all on. I looked at Jihadi François, whose weak link was his three children, two boys and a girl. It said "divorced, lost custody." Had that pushed him over the edge to hate humanity enough to kill? Next to him, Jihadi Marcus. His weak link was his brother Aidan and, beside that, women. What did it all mean?

It would take all night for me to read the rest, so I arranged it neatly and put it in the file. Then I rifled the cabinet and came to Fisher, Karen. I took a deep breath. This was it; no more mystery. Did I really want to know? Yes, I decided, and pulled my file. There was my DD214 that discharged me from the Navy in 2013.

Medical discharge due to pregnancy. They had no right to have my personal information like that. Then I picked up the letter. It was addressed to me from Steven and was dated a month before. It had been sliced up at the top. I sat down and leaned the wall adjacent to the file cabinet.

I'd met Steven in Afghanistan. He was a photojournalist and was injured when the first vehicle in the convoy he traveled with hit an IED. He was in the hospital, sitting there making shadow puppets for a sick kid in the bed next to him. He seemed so removed from the cruelties of war. I was his nurse.

He wore a boyish grin when I'd bandaged up his arm. He was cute in that studious Clark Kent way covering up Superman. He asked me to smile and showed me the pictures he took of the Afghan kids. But of all the photos, my favorite was the photo of him taken by a soldier.

The picture that was worth a million words. I'd traced his image as he knelt down and handed granola bars to a group of smiling kids. And the photo taken maybe minutes later, where he raised his hand smiling toward the photographer. He looked happy. He wore brown cargo pants with all those pockets to hold pens and camera and notebook and stuff for the kids. The black and white photos he took made me want to cry because they were the only beautiful things I'd seen in the war.

I loved his mussed hair and the stubble on his chin, which he rubbed against my cheek. He looked like he'd just rolled out of bed in the clothes he'd worn the night before without putting in hair gel. The man who was at home in a circle of kids made me want to take him in my arms. He knew what was really important.

He'd come to the hospital in Bagram several times bringing coffee or a desert flower. I couldn't imagine what I'd done to deserve such a guy. The day before he left, he gave me a photo of myself. One I didn't know he'd taken. I was looking off lost in thought. The picture hid my uncertainty about my future. My loneliness in Afghanistan.

And when he left, his emails kept me excited about getting off work to get on-line. And when I'd finally gone home for leave, he'd been at the airport with a big "Welcome Home" sign.

I'd felt I knew everything about this man when we finally made love. When I got pregnant, I exited the Navy. A miscarriage followed, but Steven had moved in with me by then. I often wondered if he regretted that. Had he only been there because of the baby that never was?

Without the Navy and with a shattered dream of being a nurse, I finished my teaching credential. I thought I'd left the injured and dying behind, not knowing more waited in a high school where I was supposed to be safe.

I opened the letter:

"When I met you it was like a glimpse of a silver object at the bottom of the ocean. Waves washing over but it shines all the way to the top. I have to pick it up, look at it and see what makes it shine. You were inserting an IV in an unconscious patient in Craig Joint Theater Hospital. And there I was a lowly reporter for the Sacramento Bee with a superficial slash to the biceps. Your blond bob swayed in front of your face covering your intense brown eyes. Something murky and gray lingered behind those eyes. Something you'd buried and never wanted to bring to the light again. I looked to the left hand for the wedding ring first but seeing none I knew I had to seek you out to see what made you shine through the bottom of the hell I had volunteered to cover, Operation Enduring Freedom.

After your fingertips played over my skin as you applied the gauges over my cut, I wanted to touch you back.

You left me there on that cot, called to another emergency and I grabbed my camera to capture a photo of a little kid who had probably lost his right leg to a land mine. As the sun shone through the room I made the kid laugh with a few shadow puppets. I didn't notice you watching until I looked up and saw the smile on your face. I knew right then I had to make you smile for the rest of your life.

It was somehow easier there.All I had to do was show up with some chocolate I had swiped from the care packages that arrived daily to the USO or a desert flower and you returned that smile to me. I stole a kiss under a full moon and you kissed me back. It shocked me that with all those heroes you choose me. Maybe I was just safe.

I knew right then and there I loved you. I forgot about that murky darkness that lingered behind those dark eyes. It is funny how safe you can feel in someone when war wages around you. I got lost in your thighs and the curve of your back. Maybe I believed I was enough to take away the dark. But I can't make you smile anymore. I hope you find your way back and if you do I will be waiting in the light."

Tears sprang to my eyes. I messed up again and hurt an innocent man. I was a villain. I threw the letter back in the file

I shoved the DD-214 behind the others. The second page was my college transcripts from the University of Maryland, the satellite campus in Bagram, Afghanistan, and my last year at UCLA. Highlighted were the three classes in Spanish I took and my grades of A.

Simmering, I thought, Where was the privacy act? I hadn't given them permission to get my transcripts. Was nothing sacred? And page three had a photo of me from Monroe High School's yearbook. Next to it was a reprint of the picture labeled with another name, Maria Sanchez, born Madrid, Spain, raised in Arizona, 26. Target: Aidan. Who was—?

A thump rose from the door, and my gaze shot in that direction. Owen filled the frame. I sucked in a breath.

"Interesting reading?"

I resisted the impulse to gather up the pages and shove them back in the file. "I... I... " Act pissed. "I'm supposed to be born in Madrid and kill a man named Aidan?"

He laughed. "That's why a little knowledge is a dangerous thing."

"Really? That's why you forget to tell us anything." I stood up and gathered the file together. Walking toward him, I slapped the file into his six-pack abdomen. "You can forget about me murdering anyone." I felt sick. I needed to get away to think.

He grabbed my arm as I passed him in an attempt to go back to my cage. Glaring at his hand clutching mine as if I could burn a hole in it, I avoided eye contact. "You don't have to kill anyone," he said. "You're the bait."

"The bait?" I gulped air. "Oh, that sounds so much better." I pulled away, but his grip didn't falter. "Let me go."

"We need to lure him into a hotel room where our people can pick him up."

"And how am I supposed to do that? I don't even speak Spanish."

He sighed and released my arm. His hand went for my neck. I flinched. What, was he... His fingers curled around the chain of his dog tags. I'd forgotten I'd slipped them over my head for safekeeping. His touch was warm, and I shuddered at the memory of his touch just an hour earlier. "Sit down," he said as he slipped the tags from my neck.

I walked to the chair as Owen rounded the desk. But as a silent protest for being bossed around, I leaned a hand on the chair and stood.

He shook his head and smiled in the "Are you serious?" expression that was becoming familiar. Then he opened the file. "How far did you read?"

"Something about my going to Madrid and my target being Aidan. Then you said I'm bait."

He signed and rubbed his eyes, suddenly looking older than his thirty... wait a minute, how old was he? I'd figured he must be a few years older than Steven. Maybe thirty-one or thirty-two. "Air strikes cause a lot of collateral damage. Too many innocents die."

I nodded. I could understand that. Hadn't my whole school of kids and teachers been taken out just to make the population feel terror?

"But these jihadists are well insulated from attack, so what choice do we have?" He looked up at me, and when I nodded, he went on. "We have to go after those closest to them. People who can get to them without taking out civilian populations. Just imagine if we had stopped Muhammed Johnny in Lerdo before he had a chance to preach his shit to the inmates who were stupid enough to listen or just wanted an excuse to kill."

I sat down slowly. That would have saved my students. My friends. I thought about Carol Jennings. She was a second-year teacher, new like me, the closest teacher to me at school. She was out sick the day of the attack. She'd called me days after. Left a few messages for me to call back, but what could I tell her? She'd cry about the losses, and I'd still wonder why me or why didn't I do something, anything? I couldn't face my friend knowing what I did. So even a friend who didn't die was lost to me. More collateral damage.

"You've met Duck Young?"

"What's that?" It sounded like a new form of martial arts or something.

"Who. 'Who's that,' you mean," He waited a beat. "The Korean kid. Computer hacker?"

Oh, I remembered the guy who sat with the Indian abortion clinic bomber. "No, but I've seen him."

"He's compiled lists of information on our bad actors." Bad actors was a term used mainly in the military for bad guys, probably because they acted badly, or so I guessed.

"Aidan's brother Marcus is a jihadist, and they stay in contact. We need you to get to Aidan."

"How?" And more importantly, what then?

"Aidan has a weakness for high-class escorts, and we're going to send you to Madrid to dangle you in front of him."

Dangle me, pimp me out. Oh my God, that was why Owen had come to my cell to try out the merchandise—get a peek at the goods. On-the-job training. Bile burned my throat. I sucked in a breath and rose quickly. I wanted to be sick. How could I have been so stupid? So lonely, so pathetic. My cheeks burned and without thinking about it, I stormed over to him and whipped back my hand to slap. He bolted upright and caught my hand.

"You need to watch that temper."

"You're an ass," I spat out. Snatching back my hand, I turned to run out the door.

"Wait," he said. Now he'd apologize. Beg for my forgiveness. Despite my anger I spun back in time to catch the peanut butter sandwich missile headed for my face. "Tomorrow you start language classes and Miss Manners Charm School."

"Obviously you aren't the teacher," I said before fleeing.

Jerk. What a cold, cold ass. As if I'd spent all my tears, I didn't cry. I gritted my teeth and chopped down that sandwich like I was back in basic training and had five seconds to eat. Then I gave my pillow more punishment.

New Recruit

I woke in the dark, my ears perked to voices. I rose and rushed for the bars. A woman's voice. Angry but incomprehensible words. One of the jailers, I guess, said, "Just keep moving." And then scuffling of feet, and in the low night light I saw two figures emerge, a jailer and a woman twisting and jerking in the glare of his flashlight.

Her skin was bronze. Disheveled hair covered her face. She reared around and spat toward him. He jumped back and shoved her. "This job is getting old." A third voice still shadowed by the dark, but distinctly familiar, laughed. Owen. The jailer slammed the metal door closed, and I saw the first occupied cell in my line of vision.

His key ground in the lock before he turned and disappeared. I strained to see the new recruit through the bars. Her tanned hands wrapped around the bars, and she shook them.

I played the only game I could in the prison: guess the recruit's history and purpose for being with Department G. She must be a jihadist or a mark. She was obviously from Afghanistan. Was she a jihadist's family member? Wife maybe? She cursed and yelled in a language I didn't understand. It was hours before she was quiet enough for me to sleep.

At breakfast, I stood in line next to George. Ahead of us, the air filled with the sound of shoving and foot stomping. The new woman, who looked Arabic and might have been in her late twenties, pushed into Daisy. As the newcomer's face reddened, the pink puckered scar on her neck darkened. She puffed out her chest so she looked as powerful as Daisy without the obvious muscles. Their voices rose over the din, but Daisy's words were the only ones I understood as she called the newcomer a "bitch" and a "hoe."

Daisy threw her arms up and shoved the newcomer. The newcomer flew back into the small table at the opening to the kitchen. The tub of silverware on the table slid from it and bounced on the floor. Metal crashed like cymbals clanging and skidded across the floor. Recruits backed up, and Duck Young stepped on my foot.

Owen and Harry—I still didn't know his real name—appeared from nowhere and maneuvered themselves behind the fighters. With fluid ease, the men threaded their powerful arms under the combatants' armpits and wrapped their fingers around the back of each fighter's neck. Daisy and the newcomer flayed their feet out, kicking at each other.

"Stand down," Owen yelled. I felt a flutter of excitement. Good luck with those two, Owen.

The women stopped struggling, and Owen and Harry let go of their necks in favor of keeping a hand on their shoulders, herding them toward the door to Owen's office. As he passed me, he met my eyes but quickly averted his. Apparently, I wasn't the only one who needed Miss Manners Charm School.

On the floor sat the newcomer's shoe. It must have fallen off when they fought. "Wait here. I think Jasmine lost her shoe," I told George, giving the newcomer a name out of Aladdin. I ducked out of line and went for the Birkenstocks-style shoe.

"Jasmine?" George asked, but I ignored him, overjoyed with my excuse to follow Owen and eavesdrop. I doubled back to the door of the offices the four had been swallowed by. Taking a deep breath, I pushed through the door and waited, holding up the shoe as if it was my hall pass.

No one stood in the hall. They'd already entered Owen's office and closed the door. Loud voices penetrated the walls. I proceeded to the door. Behind it, Daisy said, "I don't know who this Iraqi girl thinks she is but—"

"Kurdish." Jasmine's accent held a gravelly tone. "I'm Kurdish. You stupid American pig."

"Who you calling a pig, camel jockey?"

"Stand down," Owen said. "You're both giving me a headache. Each of you has a vital role in stopping terrorism. You both have a vested interest in stopping ISIS. I don't care if you don't braid each other's hair and gossip about boys all night, but you won't kill each other. We have a common interest here. So put aside your little squabble and avoid each other. Got it?"

"Fine with me," Daisy said, and I imagined her crossing her arms and turning her back.

"Okay, dismissed," Owen said, and I realized I needed to do something. I looked at the sandal in my hand and the door. I imagined chucking the sandal at the first person to exit and hightailing it out of there. The thought that it might be Owen made me laugh. Instead, I froze, my heart racing. I didn't want Owen to see me eavesdropping. I back-pedaled three giant steps before the door opened. I was caught. Daisy came out first.

"What the hell are you doing here?" she asked. I pointedly ignored her and held up the shoe as Jasmine exited.

"Did you lose a shoe?" I asked her as she walked behind Daisy.

She looked down at her feet. "Yes, thank you." Her words seemed to come from her nose.

Owen's head leaned around hers. He glared. I waited for Jasmine to take it from me before I pivoted and pushed out of the hallway.

Kurdish. Hadn't I heard about how the Kurds were fighting in Kobani? This woman wasn't swaddled in a burka, and she looked similar to a picture of an Israeli freedom fighter I'd seen on television. Maybe I could talk to her and find out more.

I walked beside her a moment back into the mess hall. Then I extended my hand. "I'm Karen. Who are you?"

She looked at my hand without taking it. "My name is Fatima," she spoke in a guttural British tongue, as if American English was foreign.

"Welcome to Department G. Do you know why you're here?"

"Not really," she said. "I was visiting my uncle in Florida, and the police came. They found weapons, and I was taken. But this place is no jail."

"You speak English well. Where are you from?"

She gave me a look as if to ask if I was joking. "Kurdistan," she said. "Near Iran and Turkey."

"Fisher," Owen said, halting me in my tracks.

I wanted to say, "Yes, Master Sergeant Kafferdy." Instead, I swallowed the sarcasm and answered with an impotent, "Yes."

"Report to room seven for language training." Room seven was next to his room in the back hallway that had nine rooms. Owen's room was number nine.

I spent my day doing PT and listening to Spanish in headsets in a room where the Indian and my new friend Fatima sat. By watching their lips, I knew they weren't listening to Spanish. That made me wonder about their missions and wish I could confiscate Owen's key again to quench my curiosity in his files.

In the afternoon, all trainees had self-defense training, and as if by design, Owen called Daisy to spar with Fatima.

The room seemed to hold a collective breath of excitement as Fatima kicked off her sandals and blew on both palms. She cupped her hands and circled Daisy, who bowed her head and scanned Fatima's midsection as if searching for a spot to land a punch.

As if a bell rang, the two leapt at each other, and soon they had shoved each other's heads in a head lock. As sweat dropped on the mat, they grunted, each attempting to land a kidney blow. Fatima gritted her teeth and grimaced.

Owen blew a whistle, but the women didn't separate. Daisy shuffled her feet and seemed to lift Fatima and twirl her so her feet thumped on the mat.

"Break it up," Owen said, but the women didn't separate. He walked to them and grabbed a handful of hair from each, snapping their heads back. The women let go of each other and grabbed at Owen's hands.

Owen let them go with one word, "Sit."

Daisy glared at Fatima and walked across the circle toward Young and the Indian dude. Fatima walked in the opposite direction toward George and me. Heat emanated from her skin like a frying pan. Her limbs quivered as she stooped to snatch up her sandals and sat cross-legged next to me. I smiled at her, and she nodded but her lips remained a tight line.

"Fisher," Owen said. I groaned inwardly. In the six self-defense classes I'd been forced to attend, I thought I'd picked up at least something. So, sighing, I climbed to my feet wondering who he'd pit me against.

But he didn't move to the side or call another trainee's name. He grabbed my arm. Jerk.

Resisting the urge to pull back, I leaned in and pushed down so his grip broke. He grabbed my shoulder. I ducked and twisted his hands off. Finally, he went for my neck. I bent my chin, turned my head, and butted my crown into the soft flesh of his neck. At the same time, I bent my knee to make contact with his groin. His wrist got there first and he pushed my knee away.

Bouncing away, I stayed on my tiptoes. Owen smiled at me. "So you have learned something."

"Yes. Must be Miss Manners Charm School." I heard George laugh and Owen smirked.

"Okay. Come here." He motioned me forward with a flip of his fingers.

When I was inches from him, he clutched my hips with his hands. His thumb played with the skin over my pelvis bones. "Come on, baby. You know you want it."

I felt strangely aroused and embarrassed at the same time. He was telling everyone in the room he'd slept with me. I felt my cheeks get hot and I tried to jerk my hips from his grasp but his fingers tightened. "What's a matter? You shy?" He rubbed the stubble of his chin over my cheek.

"Cut it out," I yelled.

"I like the wild ones." The ass must be embarrassed by my Miss Manners comment and was paying me back. I looked toward George whose mouth was opened, his buck teeth protruding in what could only be described as a bewildered look.

Screw this. I stomped down where Owen's foot was, but he moved it. Then I was pressed against him. Guilt spread over me. Wasn't this exactly what I'd wanted on this very mat days earlier? Furious, I slammed my hands down on his wrist. They held tighter. Taking a deep breath, I stepped in closer ignoring the hardness I felt under his loose martial arts pants and with a push from beneath, dislodged his hands, stepping back and freeing myself.

"Okay," Owen said. He turned to the class. "It isn't enough to be physically prepared. You can't let your attacker get under your skin or in your head. Stay mentally strong. It's important to stay cool no matter what your attacker says."

Shaking, I went to the empty spot between Fatima and George and sat. I avoided eye contact with Owen and looked at the mat until class ended.

I walked with Fatima and George to the mess when Owen called, "Fisher, my office."

"What now?" I asked.

"Perhaps a private lesson," Fatima said. When I glared at her, I saw she smiled.

"Funny."

"Lighten up, Karen," George said. "He was just demonstrating what you might hear from an attacker. Proving a point about mental toughness."

"I didn't see him making a fool out of you," I snapped at George.

"Don't think I'm his type, is all," George said. "But I wouldn't mind going a round with Fatima here."

"Bloody leave me alone. I wouldn't shag you if you were the only bloke standing." Fatima moved away from him as I turned to go the other way, toward Owen.

Part of me wanted Owen to close the door and try to take me in his arms. I'd slap him first and make him apologize. He'd kneel on the carpet and beg for my forgiveness. Then I'd make him kiss his way from my toes to my face. I felt my cheeks getting hot again.

He'd disappeared behind the door before I got there. I took a deep breath. Get a hold of yourself. He couldn't know how much I wanted him. Then I opened the door to walk in. We weren't alone.

A woman dressed in a black suit accented with a peach blouse stood in front of his desk. She reeked of flowery perfume I couldn't identify because I didn't wear anything besides a few Victoria's Secret hand creams and body sprays. I felt dumpy in my gray sweats as I stared enviously at her Prada pumps and fishnet stockings.

"Fisher, this is Louise." She even had a first name. Was Owen with her? Jealousy gripped me as I imagined them together. Then anger at how he could have led me on. But Louise was sort of a spinster great-aunt's name. "Or you can call her Miss Manners," Owen snorted through his upturned nose. "Louise, meet your Maria Sanchez. Can you do anything with her?"

Do anything with me? I narrowed my eyes as the well-put-together Louise circled me. She "tsked" and "tutted" with her tongue as she walked a circle around me first one way and then the other.

Then with as much charm as a snake, she said, "Put out your hands." She lightly drew her candy-apple-colored nails over my palms, then inspected the back of my hands. "Mamma Mia, what have you brought me? She bites her nails." Her accent sounded French , and she looked at Owen, once again talking about me as some insignificant problem.

Fantasies of flooring this woman with a shove and well-placed leg flitted through my mind, but in the end I just snatched my hands back.

"Take off the footwear," she ordered, and in an act of defiance I struck the rubbery heel of each tennis shoe to the floor and used my toes to peel the shoes off. I smiled. See what your trained monkey can do.

After I'd stripped the socks off, she looked down at my feet and jumped back like I had some contagious foot fungus. "We have some work to do, and the hair will need my attention, too." She spoke to Owen as if the trained monkey had no say in the matter.

"When do you need the miracle to transpire?" Louise said rolling the "r's" off her tongue. Did Owen find that accent seductive?

"We roll in three days," Owen answered. So that was it. I traveled in three days. I was supposed to speak native Spanish in three days. I was supposed to lead a guy to his death in three days.

THE TRANSFORMATION

The third floor, above where my cell was located , hid an open floor that housed a makeshift beauty salon. I sat at the sink while my hair was washed. At a chair fashioned to recline like a dentist's chair, I had my eyebrows plucked and my legs and bikini line waxed. Under a row of hair driers, I waited for the streaks of blond weaved through my brunette hair to dry. At a makeshift wardrobe, I stood while a tailor pinned a crimson dress up and cinched it at the waist. I got stuck twice and yelled, "I'm not a damn pin cushion! Watch it," which the tailor completely ignored. Then my toes and nails were filed, filled, and lacquered. I looked down and admired my feet. Not bad. I'd probably pay a fortune for that kind of treatment at any salon .

Louise spoke in clipped orders as she asked me to walk the catwalk wearing first a black cocktail dress and then a saffron one. I also received two pairs of designer jeans and button-down shirts.

Most of it I didn't mind as I hadn't been able to wear anything but gray sweats for over a week, and the massaging of my feet felt great. But when Louise made me walk back and forth as she yelled, "Keep your head straight. Dip your chin. No, no, no. That's not the way to move your hand. Your hand is not a limp mackerel," I had to bite my lip to avoid balling it up and demonstrating that it was a weapon. In response, she said, "And stop chewing on your lip. You'll get lipstick on your teeth."

I was allowed to choose my own shoes, and I went for the low-heeled black and red pumps I'd preferred at school due to the amount of walking I did each day. Louise, however, snapped her fingers and said, "Put them back." She made a big show of rolling her eyes. Then she grabbed her head like she had a headache instead of being the cause of my headache. She pointed at a zebra-striped and candy-apple-red pair of stilettos. Well, seriously, they did look good, but how would I ever run away from a bad guy in them?

After hours of prep, I had my photo taken. Louise explained it was for my passport picture.

Armed with my new wardrobe and look, I went back to my cell. I was about to change back into my sweats to eat dinner when Owen filled the frame of the cage's door. His eyes lit on the fishnet stockings, and I saw his Adam's apple plummet as his eyes traveled to my waist and linger on my cleavage.

"Uhm… uh… " Then his eyes went to my lacquered lips and powdered face all the way to my mascaraed eyelashes before he said, "Louise wants me to remind you that"—he sucked in an audible breath—"that you need to wear your dresses and heels unless you're sleeping. To, well, get used to them." I felt the same flutter in my abdomen I always felt around him but suddenly I realized I had the upper hand. I knew if we were alone and I had him in my room, I could drive him crazy for a change, not the other way around. I couldn't banish the smug smile from my face.

Payback time. "Okay, thanks." I'd tried for causal and dismissive and hoped I'd succeeded. Raising my well sculptured eyebrows, I asked, "Is that all?"

He seemed cemented to the floor until he ducked his head and said, "Yes," before pivoting and disappearing.

Typical man. Dress up in fishnet stockings and stilettos and they become salivating dogs. However, now I had to get through dinner dressed different from everyone else.

As the clang sounded for dinner, I stepped out of my cage as if tiptoeing over land mines. Descending the stairs, my heel got caught in the grating, and I nearly toppled down the remaining steps. Red faced, I straightened, brushed my hands over the dress, and jiggled my heel until the shoe dislodged.

George didn't close his mouth until I stood in front of him glaring and Daisy gave me a look that might have been a death beam before turning away in disgust. For days I'd wanted to wear something more form fitting than the sweats, but at that moment I wished more than anything to put them on again and blend in.

Fatima sidled up to me. "What is this that you are wearing?"

"Haven't you guys ever seen a dress and heels?" I muttered.

"Yes, but not on you," George said.

"Maybe a better question, why are you wearing a dress?" Fatima asked.

George turned around in the line and refused to move forward until I said, "Because they want me to for my mission. Besides"—now I took on a defensive tone—"why don't you wear sweats like the rest of us?" Fatima had worn the same dusty cargo pants and cotton shirt since she'd arrived four days before.

"No one should tell me how to dress," she explained.

"What's your mission?" George asked, staring at my cleavage.

"Move ahead; you're holding up the line," I said, even though we were at the end of it and because there were only seven trainees, it really didn't matter.

We sat away from everyone else but still received glances. Even Middle Eastern guy, who didn't look at anyone, stared. "So." Fatima bent close. "What is it?"

"No, you tell me your story first." A smile played over my lips. I could ransom a story as good as the next guy.

"I told you. I was visiting my uncle in Florida, and bomb-making equipment was found in his basement." That story worried me a little, as it was the second account of bombs in the group, the first being the abortion clinic bomber.

"Why were you in Florida?" I asked.

George's gaze, which had been ping-ponging between us, settled on Fatima. She smiled. "Do you know what is going on in my country?"

"I see the gist of it on the news," I answered.

"We get fired on daily. I was in Kobani trying to fight off ISIS."

"You're all Muslims. Why are you fighting them?" I asked, knowing that all Muslims weren't alike but wanting an explanation from a participant.

"I'm a Shia, and those animals don't respect our right to recognize the caliph—that's a religious leader—that we choose. Also, my uncle came to America to live, and my parents sent me to visit him on holidays and in summer. I know English. I went to school sometimes in London as well. But ISIS does not believe a woman like me should dress as I do or think or fight."

"What about your family?" I asked.

At the question Fatima's lips buckled. She didn't look at us when she spoke. "The bombing hit the place we were hiding, and my brother... " She didn't say anymore. I looked away from the tears standing in her eyes.

"So," George interrupted the silence. "Why the fancy duds, Karen?"

"I'm going to a party," I answered. "Do you know what you're doing here yet?"

"They want me to develop a drug that makes a person susceptible to hypnosis."

"Why?" I asked, thinking about the movie Telefon again, which then and forever warped my favorite Robert Frost poem.

"They just said they want to make people susceptible to suggestions of peace. I can live with that."

"These animals will never live in peace." Fatima's face contorted as she spat out the words. "They only understand war." Her voice and eyes were rock hard.

"So what do you have in mind to stop them?" I asked.

"I am to get captured, then I will set off a bomb and kill the leaders," she said and took another bite of her spaghetti. I searched her face for the punch-line. Surely she hadn't just said she was going to volunteer to die for the cause. But she didn't say anymore. Tomato sauce leaked from the corner of her mouth. I imagined it to be blood.

"But won't that mean that you... ?" and I stopped. How could I go on and ask if she was on a suicide mission.

Instead, I owed them my explanation, which I whispered, somewhat shamed by Fatima's confession. "I'm going to Spain to get some guy to turn on his jihadi brother."

George nodded. "In that, you could probably get him to turn in the whole lot of them."

I smiled wanly because I wasn't doing what Fatima was brave enough to do. I wasn't going to risk my life. I had hid when the terrorists came, and now, unlike Fatima, I hid behind a dress and heels to trap a man who might be able to get us to his brother.

The next day I was relieved to put on my sweats for PT. Owen wasn't on the floor pushing us to stretch. He didn't go out on the run with us. In fact, Harry spoke his first words to me. "Fisher. Get changed and go to the language lab." Where was Owen? I was about to embark on my mission, and he wasn't there to let me know what to expect. I fumed.

Two days until the countdown to Spain, and the next day Owen was an AWOL again. I ignored the yells from Harry, who still hadn't told us his name, and stormed Owen's office. Turning the handle proved futile. He'd locked himself in. My heart hammered as Harry hastened down the hall to stop me. "Open up, Kafferdy," I yelled. "I know you're in there."

Harry pulled on my arm to usher me away. I shrugged him off as the door opened. Owen had turned his back before I looked in the dark room. There were cell phones on his desk. Was one mine? I pushed into the office. "You can't be back here, Fisher," Harry complained.

"It's okay," Owen said, and Harry left. "Close the door." Owen sat down.

I recognized my phone. "That's mine. You have my phone." I snatched it up.

"You can't get reception in here anyway. The walls," he said, rubbing his bloodshot eyes. Stubble of maybe two or three days darkened his angular chin, and his clothes looked slept in.

I pressed a button to turn my phone on. The battery icon reported power at 13 percent. Four new text messages and three missed calls popped up on the screen, but only one new voicemail. Maybe I wasn't missed that much. Who could blame anyone?

"A charger?" I hadn't had one in my purse, but surely he'd have one. He opened a drawer and slid one over to me. It fit my phone. I looked at him as he scanned some documents like I was invisible. Jerk. I crawled around his desk to find an outlet for the charger.

Steven had called. I pushed the voicemail code in. "Karen, are you ever going to call me back? Well, this is message number... I don't know, a hundred? Call your mom and then call me. If you want to. Bye." Anger.

I glared toward Owen. One hundred messages and only three missed calls. He'd read my others. How had he gotten my code? Then I remembered Duck Young, hacker jackass. I pressed the button to get my saved voicemails. The next message started, "This is Doctor Wells's office. You missed your dental appointment. I heard on your answering machine you are in rehab in Mexico, but you needed to give us twenty-four hours' notice. I'm sorry, but there will be a thirty-two-dollar cancellation charge." And no cleaning for another year unless Department G had a health plan.

The two following messages asked me if I wanted to renew my subscription to Entertainment Weekly and the library letting me know the book I'd reserved, The Alchemist, was in. I groaned. I'd been the number ten requester, and now I'd lost my place in line. What else had I missed?

More messages from Steven angry about not hearing from me. Until I got to his initial message: "Karen, I'm worried. You never told me you were going to Mexico for rehab. I had to break into the house to make sure you weren't lying in a puddle of your own vomit. Call me. I love you." My eyes welled up with tears. "I hope you're getting the help you need. I watered the cactus. I wish you'd call. Your mom's worried. She keeps calling to ask what's up and why I don't know anything. Okay, well, call, okay?"

I jolted out of my seat. "You listened to my private messages?"

Owen didn't look at me. "Had to. We put out a message explaining you were in rehab, but you still got calls."

"Those were private. I need to call him and my mom and let them know I'm okay."

"That's why we don't let you have the phone. You're in training, and we don't get much service anyway." He looked up at me. I felt so much heat in my cheeks I thought I might spontaneously combust. He shook his head at me. "Okay. If you have to, use my phone to call your boyfriend." Was it just my imagination, or did his voice rise at the word "boyfriend"?

I grabbed up his phone but then lowered it to the desk. What could I tell Steven? "Hi. I'm fine. No, rehab's great." Lie, lie, lie. "Coming home? Well, that's a good question." Where is home anymore? Who am I now? Someone who has sex with a stranger. At that I felt a tingle between my legs. Someone who still wants to screw this asshole in front of me.

I put down the phone, and Owen looked up with what appeared to be a sneer on his lips. "I'll text him later," I said. "In privacy." That earned me a snort.

I wanted to slap Owen. Instead, I sat back down and read my texts. There were more than four I hadn't read. Steven texted me saying he loved me and we needed to talk the moment I got home. My lips buckled. What had changed? I hadn't had nightmares here, but that was because I was doing something. And because I'd had no alcohol, but would I need a drink the moment I had to deal with people asking how I was, psychiatrists making me relive it, and so-called friends' morbid fascination with death? Many of the texts were from those friends.

Kathy: "Hey, girl. Reporters still at your home? They questioned me about your sudden disappearance from the interview. Where'd you go? You just disappeared. Anyway check out the LA times for my article about you and me. Bye now BFF. I'll keep you posted on book club. We're reading some book called "Sweetness in the Belly" about some girl from, IDK, Afghanistan or something. Hugs and kisses."

"Sweetness in the Belly" was about a girl from Persia in the sixteenth century. I'd picked it because I'd heard it was good. So the publicity whore had got herself in the public eye. I wanted to read her interview, see what BS she'd written, but I didn't want to read it. I had other things on my mind.

"Your mom's a real trip," Owen said.

I shot him a glare. "Pardon me?"

"Yeah. You didn't get to her messages yet? She's upset that you embarrassed the whole family on live television. She wants to know why you didn't let her help you get into the Betty Ford Center for drug rehab in Palm Springs."

"Shut up." I rose and walked over to him. "And what is your mother like, Happy Days?"

"No, dead."

That forced me to rock back on my heels for a moment. "Well, mine's alive and wants to help me."

"Well, that makes two of us."

"How are you helping me? You have been AWOL for two days. I go to Madrid in a day, and you aren't even around."

He pointed to the paperwork on his desk. "I've got paperwork."

Screw him. I didn't need to put up with this. He didn't want me. I didn't need him. As I forced my feet to the door, he said, "Karen. Don't get close to anyone here. We have a job to do, and people will just get in your way."

He meant me. I would get in his way. In the way of what was important to him. His mission. I swallowed the lump in my throat. "Bullshit." I turned from the door and walked around his desk. I pressed close to him. So close, the knee of my nylons touched his chair.

He turned around, making me jump back, and to steady me he grabbed my leg. His face got red, and he moved his hand up so it played with the hem of my dress. Then he stood, raising my dress to my waist. "Is this what you want?" He looked at my lips. His voice grew husky. "You want me to bend you over my desk and take you right here?"

I brought my hand inches from his face before he grabbed it and pulled me into him. I felt the hardness under his jeans, and my breath quickened. "No, I have a boyfriend, remember?"

"Yeah, is that right? Sounds like you two are real tight."

"Nosey, eavesdropping—" I couldn't finish the rest because his lips covered mine, choking off the word. I shuddered and forced my tongue in his mouth.

The chair flew back as he shoved me to the wall so my back was pinned. His hands gripped my hips and he groaned.

"Owen," Louise's voice sounded through the door. I spun around and stepped away from Owen as the door flew open. We all stood with our mouths open. Louise's grip tightened around the door handle. She stammered. "Well... I'll... I'll just come back later." She started to close the door.

"No, no," Owen said. "We're done here. She was just leaving." And with that he dismissed me again. He turned from me and picked up the overturned chair.

Embarrassed and more pissed than ever, I went for the door. I shoved past Louise. "Excuse me." When the door closed with that familiar sucking sound, I leaned against the wall outside his office to straighten out my dress. I touched my lips and felt the raw area where his lips had meshed with mine. My lipstick was probably a mess. Then I stopped at the voice.

"Owen, do you know what you're doing?"

"Yeah. That? That was nothing. You didn't see anything. I'm handling it." I imagined him rubbing the back of his neck. Nervous.

"Well, looks to me like you're in over your head with her."

"No way. She's nothing to me."

I bit my lip and my eyes watered.

"Really," Louise said.

Yes, really? Nothing. I was nothing to him. I fumed with humiliation.

"What did you come in for?" Owen asked.

"Oh, yes. There are reports," Louise said. "There's talk about a possible attack on Paris." ISIS in Paris too? I trembled. Another attack. Surely we couldn't go to Madrid with ISIS attacks so close in France.

"What?" Owen asked. "What sources?"

"Our network."

"When?"

"We don't know. Should we reschedule?"

"No. I think we're still safe for Madrid, then we'll concentrate on François in France. I think the timing will be okay. I'll make a few calls to be sure everything is a go."

I wanted to stay and resume what Owen and I started. But I turned before Louise could catch me outside the door.

Instead of leaving, I ducked around a corner and let Louise pass. When the hall was deserted again, I patted down my hair and started toward Owen's office again.

Suddenly I heard a bang in the office—a slam that sounded like a piece of furniture hitting the wall and then a low guttural yell: "God, I'm so tired." Then another slam and a grunt of pain. "Damn, damn, damn."

I couldn't enter his office now. I ran for the mess door and entered the cafeteria. Harry looked at me and then at the cell phone still pressed in my hand. "Where'd you get that?" he asked, and I pushed past him to the stairs leading up. "Fisher, where you going? You have language lab."

"Screw language lab and screw you too, Harry."

"Name's not Harry," he said as I hit the top step and turned to return to my cage.

FIRST MISSION

The next morning, I was in a Lincoln with Owen, Harry-but-not-really-Harry, my stylist, and a driver, I had yet to name. The sun was just rising over what seemed like miles of desert. Dry, brown tumbleweed rolled over fine, thirsty dirt. I hadn't slept well, and I pressed into the seat by the window, forcing Owen into the middle. He couldn't request a different seat without making a scene, which I didn't think he'd want.

I craned my neck to see if I could spot a street sign, some hint of where we were. Not LA; too deserted. And the street was unpaved.

I started to chew a nail when Owen grabbed my hand. "Stop that." The warmth of his hand sent a spasm of warmth between my legs. I hadn't slept much because I had spent half the night hoping Owen would come to me.

Louise slung a hand over the front seat where she sat shotgun and "tsked" at me. "You have bags under your eyes. What man would want a tired-looking escort?" Owen dropped my hand.

"Should we use the hood?" Harry asked from his seat on the other side of Owen .

"No. It'll mess up her hair," Owen answered, and I realized they were discussing me. A hood! What was I, some hostage?

"I'll have to fix it anyway," Louise said.

"Excuse me, I'm right here. And I'm not putting on a damn hood. What do you take me for, some kid? I'm part of this team. You chose me, remember."

"Okay, cool it," Owen said.

The Lincoln made a bumpy turn onto a paved road. The wooden sign read, 102nd Street. 102nd street? What town, what city, what state? I needed to know where I was.

"Let's just give her a sleeping tablet," Louise said.

"No, because I'm not tired." This woman was really getting on my nerves. What was she, thirty-five years old? Forty? What gave her the right to boss me around?

"Hand me the cooler," Harry said, and Louise passed him a collapsible blue cooler. He took out a bottle of water and twisted the cap off. He passed it to Owen. Louise reached over from the front seat and produced two little white pills.

"Here, take these. They'll make things easier." Owen opened my curled fingers and pressed the pills into my palm.

"How am I supposed to go through the airport asleep?" I asked.

Out the window on Harry's side, a motel materialized. It had a dirty wooden sign that read "Ra ch Motel" hanging off a rotted post. The motel's outer walls were the color of urine and it looked abandoned.

"We're taking a private plane," Owen answered. He didn't let go of my open hand.

"Department G rich or something?" I asked, pushing back against Owen's fingers which pressed the pills toward my mouth.

"We have some very generous patrons who want peace for financial reasons," Owen explained. "Now take those and go to sleep." He dropped my hand.

I leaned next to his ear and whispered. "Say please."

His nostrils flared and he inhaled before putting his hand on my thigh. His fingers curled around my upper leg and squeezed harder than necessary. "This what you want?" His lips tickled my ear lobe. "You want me to take you right here?"

I swallowed the lump in my throat and noticed the angry red scrapes on his knuckles. My skin burned. Is that what I heard hitting the wall the day before? His nails dug into flesh, scorching me but at the same time making my stomach tingle.

My eyes watered. "Stop. I'll take them," I said, and he let go. I closed my tired eyes. I hated him. Mean dirtbag. He didn't care about me at all. He could let me go seduce some stranger without a hint of emotion. I bit my tongue to avoid a strangled cry from escaping my throat.

The last thing I heard before my head swam into a foggy sleep was Harry. "I can't wait to get out of this shithole Palmdale desert. If I never saw tumbleweed again, it would be too soon. How long to the airport?"

When I woke again, sun streamed into the window. Below me, the slippery seats warmed to the sun. A taxi? I looked around. I sat between Harry and

Louise in a backseat. Plexiglass separated me from Owen and the driver up front. The driver's eyes appeared in the rearview mirror, and he quickly looked away. I rubbed my tongue over my teeth, which felt gritty.

Squinting out the window, I saw boxy white buildings and crowds of people walking or cycling over the smooth street. I strained to see street signs. I recognized Spanish writing and the store signs. The taxi stopped in front of a six-story white hotel that looked like a castle at the top. Five colorful flags stuck like birthday candles on the top above the sign that read "Hotel Mediodia." Did that mean Hotel Middle Day? How strange.

Louise opened the door. I tapped her arm and asked, "What time is it?"

"Noon. We have ten hours to get you completely transformed. Let's go." She handed me a pair of Dea Desire white-framed sunglasses with smoky lenses. I wobbled as I stood on my heels. My legs tingled from sleep as I limped forward.

I stood in the bronze-colored lobby in front of a bank of elevators waiting for Owen to check in. Our Briggs and Riley matching suitcases lay on a velvet-lined rolling suitcase carrier. We traveled first class, for sure.

Owen came around the corner and held out a skeleton key to me. I shivered. We were really going to do this—send me in to lead a man to, what, his death? To ransom him to his brother? I didn't know how much I could trust Department G. After all, they did work underground, unrecognized by proper authorities.

BARCELONA

I stared into the mirror. Not a hair out of place. No matter how put together I felt, on the inside I shook. The minibar sat in the corner. Maybe just one. The surveillance cameras were in place as well as the bugs, but they were busy, so I didn't think they'd be monitoring it so early. And I just needed one to take the edge off. Just one. No one had to know, and it could stop—might stop—the nerves.

There were small bottles of wines and some Coke with Spanish writing. Then some whiskey and brandy... okay, the brandy would do it. I unscrewed the top with a trembling hand and took it to my lips. The burn almost immediately calmed me. But the bottle was small. The calm in my gut felt great, but it wasn't quite enough. Only one more—that's all I needed. Just one more. I took a deep breath as I unscrewed the second and drained it.

Then a thought hit me. The hotel would charge the drinks to the room. I shuddered. Okay, don't panic. I could go to the desk and pay. I put the bottles in the trash but retrieved them quickly. No, I had to hide them. I stuffed them in my purse. In the bathroom there was some mouthwash. I gargled it.

Minutes later, the phone jangled, making me jump. I picked it up. "Hello." My voice was tentative.

"Time," Owen said. "You ready?"

Louise had explained that Aidan had been exposed to a picture of me from an internet site he used. The meet was set, and he would approach me. "Yes." I put down the phone and smoothed out my skirt. I tottered a little on the heels. Just nerves, I thought, steadying myself against the chest of drawers. Okay, chin up. Remember to breathe. I can do this. I left for the hotel bar.

The mirrored wall behind the bar stretched like a mouth swallowing the room in front of it. I sidled up to one of the dozen empty crimson stools at the front bar counter. A low yellow light warmed the darkened room and contrasted with the brightly colored neon beer slogans.

Two men's heads swiveled in my direction as they slumped over their glasses of amber whiskey. Behind them sat Harry-not-really-Harry. He lowered his eyes. The mirror's reflection filled with couples of men and women in burgundy booths huddled over cocktails with rainbow-colored umbrellas or long-necked beer bottles. I ran my gaze over the reflected faces and didn't see Aidan.

"Qué quieres?" the bartender asked.

I forced my eyes from the mirror to stare at the bald, round-faced man with the kind hazel eyes. Owen had advised me to order a club soda. I swallowed the lump in my throat and with a shudder ordered sangria.

As the drink materialized in front of me, something touched my elbow. I turned to look into the green eyes of Aidan. He was handsome like a male fashion model, with an angular jaw and cheek bones and alabaster skin under brown bangs and shaggy hair that needed a scissor's attention.

"Maria," he said and passed his gaze from my fishnet stockings to my cleavage. He ordered a drink, and soon his hand found its way to my thigh. He slid his palm under my shirt, and I moved it down with a forced smile. I felt giddy. And wished Aidan was Owen and our lives were such that we could sit in a bar together.

Aidan ordered another round. Darting a glance, I saw Harry shaking his head. To hell with him. I took a swallow.

After the second sangria, Aidan said, "We will speak English because your Spanish is not as good." Then he took my glass and, placing it on the bar, said, "Let's leave this place and go to your room, no?" He licked his lips, and I felt sick.

His hand grazed my breast. "You have spilled some drink." Then he bent to lick the area while his tongue traveled to my neck.

"No. Not here. Let's go." I pushed him away. Everything swam. The world tilted as I stood. I fell into him and laughed to cover up my embarrassment.

Aidan's hand slipped over my shoulders, and he groped my crotch as we got in the elevator. He leaned into me as we rose to go to the second floor. I moved back. "Wait, what about the money?" An escort would demand money, Louise had reminded me.

Aidan stuffed a hand in his back pocket to extract a wallet. He leaned in and crammed bills in my cleavage. "No. not here," I said, but he ignored me and tried to slip my skirt to my hips. "No," I said. I laughed as I pushed him back. "We're almost at my room."

He ignored me, pulling at my skirt while burying his lips into my neck. Finally, to get him off, I kneed him in the groin. He reared back clutching the front of his pants. He let out a roar as the door to the elevator opened. "You like to fight like a tiger," he wheezed. I took my eyes off him to exit and didn't see his palm come down hard on my cheek.

I recoiled, but the sting spread over my lip and cheek. I tasted the metallic blood from my cut lip. He hurled a rough stream of curses at me. Side-stepping his doubled-over body, I got out of the elevator. I pushed on to my room, stumbling on the stiletto heels.

I dug through my clutch, and the bottles fell from my purse. The skeleton key slid through my fingers onto the shaggy gold colored carpet, and I knelt to retrieve it. Aidan's fingers grasped a handful of my hair. He yanked my neck back.

The key dug into my fingers. Rising, I clutched his wrist to get my hair free. Twisting, I used the stiletto to stab his foot. He let go of my hair. I lunged toward the door.

The key jumped in the lock. Okay, you're almost there. Calm down. I blinked to clear my vision. The key slid into the slot. Aidan's hand squeezed the back of my neck. I threw an elbow behind me. The pressure on my neck remained. I threw back a second elbow. It only grazed his side. As my vision blurred, I turned the key and the door clicked open. I fell to my knees. Crawling over the carpet, I snagged my nylons. I pushed on through the door.

Aidan grabbed at my waist, lifting me off the ground. I twisted toward him, throwing wild punches. He shoved me backward. I bounced off the edge of the bed. My tailbone slammed against the floor.

Suddenly a flutter of movement started at the doorframe. A blur of Owen's face. Aidan yelled, and the door slammed. Aidan was flipped onto the bed, and Owen forced his hands behind his back. Metal handcuffs circled Aidan's wrists. Owen heaved him to his feet.

Harry stood at Owen's side, and the two turned to shove Aidan out the door. Then I was alone. My head hurt. My face stung. I rose and kicked off the heels. I looked into the mirror at my hazy reflection. I rounded the bed to the chest of drawers. My head twirled, and I closed my eyes. My fingers wrapped around the cool wood steadied me.

Owen. He'd be furious. I'd botched up this retrieval. I was suddenly scared. He'd throw me out of Department G. Where would I go? What would I do? I couldn't live without Owen. I ran to the toilet and vomited. Mascara and eyeliner streaked my face as I bent over the sink to rinse my mouth with the hotel mouthwash. It burnt my lip.

My hands shook. I'd forgotten about my students. For a moment I'd forgotten about that day. Instead I feared the next few hours. My mouth was too dry. I gulped water from the tap.

Tears streamed down my cheeks as I opened the fridge. I knocked four bottles to the floor. And instead of water, I unscrewed a red wine. I'd ruined it. I was out, so why not drink?

I took a sip. Owen burst through the door. He was in front of me when he hit the bottle from my hand. It crashed against the wall. "Are you out of your mind?"

His knees pressed into mine. "You promised not to drink. You could have gotten yourself killed." He bent to the fridge and with one arm flung the rest of the contents to the floor. The crash of glass against metal filled the room.

I cowered on the bed and pulled my knees to my chest. My back bumped the headboard.

Owen looked at me. His hand shot out. I cringed as he brushed my lip. My tongue felt the area and licked his fingers in doing so. "Does it hurt?" he asked.

What should I say? Was he angry? Concerned? I couldn't read him. He knelt down on the bed and slid closer to me. "Are you okay?" he asked again.

I shuddered. "I'm sorry," I cried. "I'm so sorry. I don't know what happened. I was shaking and I just thought maybe one... "

He took my chin in his hand and a smirk lifted half of his mouth. Then he enveloped me in his arms. I sagged against him. His hands traveled up and down my back. "It was too soon, that's all. Too soon," he said. He loosened his grip, and I lifted my chin. "You need water and aspirin. We'll talk in the morning, okay?"

He opened a water bottle, and I obediently took two aspirin. "Will you stay?" I asked.

He sighed. "Here?" I nodded. "For a little while. Then I have to go."

Owen moved aside the sheets, and we slid in. His arm still circled my shoulders. I must have woken in the middle of the night, jolting up from a nightmare I couldn't remember. Owen's arm rested across my chest. He snored lightly as I scooted out from under his embrace.

I felt slightly unsteady, but mostly I was scared. What would happen to me now? Owen's eyes opened. "What's the matter?" he asked.

I turned from him to the window. Moving aside the curtains, I avoided looking him in the face. Colorful lights flickered over the city, making it hard to recognize it from any other busy city. "Do you want me to get out?" I hesitated. "I'm not good at this." I swallowed to keep my ever-present tears at bay.

"Do you want out?" He had moved so the heat off his hip warmed my back.

"I died in that attack on my school," I explained, surprised at the admission. "I was there that morning, but those gunmen took me with them."

"What do you mean?" Owen asked, touching my chin so I moved to look him in the eyes.

I shrugged him off. "Steven said it best. I died that day—or who I was did—and I can't get that back. No one I knew knows me anymore, and what's worse, I don't recognize me anymore."

"At least you have people who are willing to help you either way."

"Either way?" I asked.

"Whatever you decide."

"Decide. I didn't decide to disappear, and I can't get that back. No." I shook my head. "I can't go back. I can't handle anything anymore, that's why I needed a drink to steady my nerves. After it happened, I couldn't move without a drink. But who am I now?"

"You are important to our fight. It was just too soon. You can be someone who does something about what happened to you. What happened to us all in one way or another."

"Am I the girl who lures a man into my hotel room to his death? I used to be a teacher, someone who read everything. Someone who educated kids in what I thought was important, but how important is literature when the bullets ripped into their bodies? I thought my books gave the story of a common humanity. I've read hundreds of novels about suffering. But what do I know of suffering? I'm a fraud. It made sense then, but does it now? Is it still important?"

Owen looked at me. "I don't know anything about humanity. If you ask me, there is no true humanity, just a code to live by, and actions to follow to make it easier."

"What did I owe to them? What do I owe anyone? Maybe I should have died too."

"No one person is more important than the whole. That's why you can't get too close to anyone. I warned you about that."

"That's not a world I want to live in. What about people you love?"

He shook his head. "There's no one left."

And I remembered. "Your mom died," I whispered, not meaning to open an old wound.

"Yes. At childbirth." He looked at his hands.

"And your father?"

"Not much of one. A Marine. Gone more than there, and enough step-monsters to make me realize I had only myself to count on." He thrust out his chin and looked me in the eyes again.

The sadness in his eyes impelled my hand to touch his cheeks. He grabbed my hand and pressed it into his face. "I had my brothers, but an RPG ended that. I have my code. That's who I am."

"No other family?" I swallowed the fear before I asked, "A wife? Kids?"

"Made that mistake, but she realized I wasn't going to be there to hold her hand. I'm not made out for that life. And when the helo crashed, I couldn't be around her or my daughter."

"Daughter?"

"Lost custody. I'm not there and not fit. Better off without me. Wife got remarried. Someone who will stay at home. Someone who can pretend that this is a safe world as long as it doesn't touch them."

Maybe that was who I was too, now. Someone who couldn't be around people, who could shut out the dangers that were out there. But tonight I'd proven I wasn't good at taking action either. I wanted another drink to forget about it, to face the fact that I wasn't strong enough to live in either world anymore. I shuddered again.

"You cold?" he asked.

"No, just a shiver ran up my spine."

He gathered me in his arms. I felt him harden against my thigh. Then he sat on the edge of the bed. He grabbed my hand to tug me back on the bed. This time he took his time. He slowly unrolled my ruined fishnets. He unbuttoned my shirt and unzipped my skirt. Hungrily, I shoved his shirt up, but he grabbed my hands to stop me. "Wait. I'm not finished." Then he kissed my thighs and the back of my knees. When I looked at him, our eyes locked as if he were monitoring my reaction.

I shivered. He worked his way up until he lingered between my thighs. I grabbed his head and let out a yelp. He laughed and pushed me back again. This time he worked his tongue up my stomach to each nipple. "Enough," I whispered. "Do it already." My breath came in pants but he just smiled and pushed me back to nibble at my neck.

Finally, he stood over me, and I snatched his shirt, thrusting it upward. He laughed, pulling it over his head. I let my hands play over the soft fuzz of his abdomen. I touched the scar tissue in a dozen spots that rose over the smooth landscape. Then I took lips to his old wounds. Air hissed through his teeth as I kissed each one. His hands played in my hair. Then he pulled my face to his and kissed me.

Needing him, I worked the zipper of his pants. He held my nipples between his fingers, and I moaned. I dragged his boxers to his knees and took him in my mouth. He arched his back, and then, pushing me down, he entered me. He whispered, "Oh God, you're dangerous to me. Oh God, I can't stay away."

Joy pressed heavy tears in the back of my eyes. Finally, I wasn't alone. As he rocked over me, I grabbed onto his back and held on as if my life depended on it, and maybe it did.

COLLATERAL DAMAGE

Back at Department G, Fatima and Daisy were gone. Obviously, their missions were underway. The trainee dress code had changed as well. I'd kept my jeans and button-down shirts, and other trainees wore the same.

I wanted to know what was next for me, but fear—what else?—stopped me from storming into Owen's office to demand an answer. An inner voice nagged at me that I didn't belong at Department G. But what alternative did I have? My only safety came from being there and being told what foot to put in front of the other instead of drinking to keep from moving at all.

For a week, my time was filled with the routine things: cleaning, cooking, mopping, and laundry. Until I watched two suits and Owen climb the stairs to the third floor, and I knew I had to find out what was behind the doors.

I crept up the steps, looking back to make sure no one witnessed me. So far, so good. At the door, I stopped to listen. A guttural yell made me start. It sounded like matadors were sticking an enraged bull.

I clasped the door handle and hesitated before turning it. Pressing my face to the wall, I inched the door open. Light flooded out, ricocheting off the white floors. Beyond them in a reclining chair sat Aidan. He writhed and pulled against arm restraints pinning his forearms to the chair. He looked wild, with matted hair and stubble hiding his angular chin. His lips pulled back into a growl.

His fingers clenched and unclenched as if trying to dislodge an IV attached to the back of his hand. Oh God, what had I done? A moment later, his body slackened, and Owen came into view behind him. The Middle Eastern trainee—I'd named him Muhammed—shoved some papers in front of Aidan's face and spoke to him in Spanish too rapid for me to follow. Only the word muerta—"death"—left me cold. Aidan turned his head, and Owen snatched a handful of his hair, forcing his eyes in front of the pictures. The look of hatred in Owen's face squeezed my heart.

Nausea riled in my stomach. I was culpable in the torturing of this man. The media had reported on Guantanamo Bay, where Iraqi prisoners were allegedly tortured. But I hadn't personally experienced any torture, and most importantly, not at the hands of Owen.

Shaking, I eased the door shut. What had I expected? Owen was a member of Seal Team Six; of course he had to do whatever it took to safeguard our country. However, to torture this guy who was an ass, but wasn't a terrorist, was hard for me to swallow.

What if I unclamped the arm straps and let Aidan escape? I'd gotten him there, so I needed to give him a chance to leave. They'd lock the door and probably keep twenty-four-hour surveillance on him. Okay, I'd have to get Owen's dog tags, enter his office, and find a key to the room to release Aidan. But that meant seducing Owen and possibly getting rejected. And it meant stealing his keys while he slept a second time.

At dinner, my stomach clenched in a tight knot, so I slopped the spaghetti sauce from one side of my plate to another. George prattled on, "Well, where do you think Fatima is now? Do you think she did it—offed herself with a bomb?"

"I don't know." I sighed, hoping she hadn't been captured and killed or was being given an IV of drugs as I expected Aidan was.

"Hey, look who's back," George said, and I looked in the direction he pointed.

Daisy sat down. She somehow looked buffer and brighter than she had before she left. She was back, but Fatima might never be . All the death made me shake internally.

Owen cleared his throat before I noticed he stood next to us. "Fisher and Harrison, need you both in the conference room when you finish."

Before I could answer, he was gone. He hadn't been around all week, but now I'd be in the same room as him doing God knows what. My heart kicked into overdrive.

"Wonder what that's about?" George asked.

"If you're finished, let's go to the conference room and find out." I rose to empty my tray. I'd never been invited into the conference room before. Maybe it meant I was no longer a trainee but a full-fledged member of Department G.

When I opened the door, Owen lifted his head from the projector. We were alone. As if he were a string drawing me in, I started toward him, feeling the need to say something. But I stopped because George entered behind me, followed by Daisy, Muhammed, and Harry.

"Take a seat." Owen motioned toward the ten chairs hugging the conference table.

I pulled out the chair directly in front of me. George sat next to me. As soon as everyone was seated, Harry flipped the lights off.

The slide show started with a picture of a turbaned Arab man. "This is Akbar Mubaric," Owen said. I gasped. Muhammed's face filled the screen. Owen clicked to the next slide of Muhammed in a suit talking to two other men. The third slide showed the men more casually dressed in vests and surrounded by missiles. "He's responsible for dealing in weapons for a small insurgent group operating out of Bakran, Iran."

So not Muhammed. But the resemblance was uncanny. Maybe his twin? Then a thought hit me: maybe Muhammed had been kidnapped to trap his twin brother. Or—my mind raced with other stories—Muhammed could have been pardoned for the abortion clinic bombing if he trapped his brother as an offering to Department G.

Owen continued, "Akbar lives here in the US and attends a mosque in Silver Spring, Maryland." The next slide showed a white mosque with three golden balls on the center dome.

"We're going to Maryland, ladies and gentleman."

Owen picked up five red folders and passed one to Muhammed on his left, who circulated the others by the take-one-pass-it-on method to the rest of us.

Owen pointed to Muhammed. "Hassan here will be joining the mosque." So I got another name wrong. "Ross is going undercover as his wife, so both will have surveillance of Akbar. Smith and I are undercover as Akbar's driver and a cop. Harrison and Karen, uhm, Fisher, are lookouts and in case we need medics." Okay, we were playing civilians . But if he wanted us for medical reasons, chances were someone was getting hurt.

I also thought about Hassan, the abortion clinic bomber, in a mosque. Surely they weren't thinking about bombing the mosque.

I opened my folder as Owen continued. "This is an in-and-out operation. We go in, take him out in two days, and disappear. Burner phones are being distributed but not turned on until we need them." He motioned toward the bucket of cell phones at his right elbow.

The first page in my folder was a title page. The second had a paper clip attaching my Virginia driver's license. It showed my fake listed name,

Catherine Heathcliff. I looked up at Owen. Was it some sort of joke? Was my fascination with Wuthering Heights noted somewhere in my file? My stomach fluttered as I fantasized that Owen was sending me a subliminal message with the names. He was letting me know we were like the star-crossed lovers Catherine and Heathcliff. Idiot. Snap out of it. Owen was as romantic as a black widow.

"We will be residing in a patron's home while on location and will have access to his vehicles." Owen looked down at his folder. "You each have a picture of the target in your folder. Burn that image in your mind, because you won't be taking the folders with you. Daisy and Hassan will keep surveillance in the mosque, and the rest of us will be posted on the route to the dump site." Dump site? Oh God, it dawned on me that when Owen said "taking him out," he meant permanently. Not just out of commission. Dead.

"I'll be taking over for the driver that day," Owen said. "Smith and I will incapacitate him while the target is in the mosque. Then we set off the gas, dispose of him with minimal mess, and we're out."

My head swam. Lookouts, taking people out, poison gas. What was my role, exactly? As if reading my mind, Owen said, "Fisher and Harrison, you will set up surveillance in the garage. We drive in with the corpse, change the driver back out, make the switch, and split the scene. Young is working on the surveillance cameras in the parking structure. All we need you to do is put up cones and keep traffic out of that area. You'll be dressed as parking lot employees. Any questions?"

I tentatively lifted my arm into the air. I saw Daisy blow out a disgusted breath. Owen called on me.

"Why?" I asked.

"Why what?"

"Why take him out? Why not report him to the police? And if you're worried that another guy will just take his place, how will killing him prevent that?"

No one else in the room met my eyes. "Because, Fisher, the switch is Hassan for Akbar. He looks enough like Akbar, and a little surgery will take care of the rest. Once we get into their weapons trading, we can do some real damage."

George raised his hand. Owen called on him. "What clothes do we need to pack?"

"Louise has picked out some clothes for cool weather. It's almost December, and it will be cold where we're going."

December. My school had been attacked Thursday, October 22nd. I'd missed Thanksgiving. Mom would never forgive me. Would Christmas slip by as well, unobserved? And then a fantasy of buying Owen something to mark our first holiday filled me. Stupid; he'd barely talked to me since we'd returned from Spain.

VIRGINIA

The private plane that flew us to the East Coast did so in the dark of night. Five hours later, the sun lit up the interior of the plane, and I'd hardly slept. Damn the three-hour time difference anyway.

Walking out onto the tarmac, goosebumps formed under my sheer blouse, and I rummaged in my bag for a sweater. A black SUV whisked us to a mansion.

The circular drive encompassed a birdbath the size of a public kiddie swimming pool and had a statue of a naked boy peeing the water into a white stone basin. At least a dozen trees stood in front of the two-story building with four picture windows on each floor.

After we'd lugged our suitcases into the opened entrance way, I surveyed the wide staircase of marble, which could easily accommodate four people walking side by side. The railing looked brass.

"Ross and Fisher, you get the first room on the right."

Daisy echoed my surprise. "I got to bunk with her?"

We said nothing as I let Daisy pick which bed she wanted of the two queen-size, canopy-style beds.

I opened the sliding glass doors in our room and stepped outside . The rear view from our wrap-around balcony revealed a green lawn that reminded me of a golf course. A lake nestled between dozens of trees. I hadn't seen a tree in forever.

Down on the porch directly below me, Owen spoke to somebody I couldn't see. "We need to strike tonight because it's Friday. He'll be at the mosque. We'll get a few hours of sleep first."

Cigarette smoke drifted through the still, cool air up to me. I knew Owen didn't smoke, so he wasn't alone or talking on the phone. "I have studied the layout," Hassan said in his heavy accent. "I know what to do. Do you think the two new ones will be okay? I heard the girl almost blew the mission in Spain."

I sucked in a breath. Would Owen defend me? Then I felt a flash of anger. If I was such a screw up, why had they brought me at all?

"She'll be okay," Owen said. Was there a defensive edge to his voice, or had I imagined it? He continued, "She's with Harrison, and they only need to block off the top layer of parking. They'll go over their instructions before we roll." So I got the no-brainer job. "You have the hard part. Are you ready to disappear and become a double agent?"

"I'm willing to give my life to it. Inshallah."

As I turned to return to the room, a shiver ran down my spine. There it was—the distinct difference between me and everyone else at Department G. I wasn't willing to risk my life even for my students.

On her bed, Daisy lay fully dressed over the flowered comforter, her arm draped over her eyes. I pulled the sheer drapes over the window. Grabbing my overnight bag, I headed for the bathroom that opened into our room.

There was a double sink and Jacuzzi-style tub and shower. The towels were made of the plushest terry cloth I'd ever felt. I closed the door and ran hot water in the tub. Bath crystals of lavender sat next to the gold-colored spout. I poured in a handful and watched the sweet-smelling bubbles rise. Slipping out of my clothes, I sank into heaven. I pressed the jets so they churned, massaging my heavy limbs.

Despite my resolve, I began to cry. Stupid. Why? I was happy. I had a new life, and surely I could win Owen back. And now I was surrounded by more luxury than I'd ever felt. Any minute I feared I'd wake up and find myself drunk on the floor of my kitchen so lost I could never come back. Who was this girl? Where did she belong? And now I would help kill a man. He was a killer, no doubt, but something inside me ached nevertheless.

I fell asleep in the bath until a tap sounded at the door. My eyes popped open, and through fog that dulled my brain, I noticed the water had become cool and the whirlpool had stopped so the bubbles had turned into dead, slippery splotches.

"Fisher." Owen's voice. "You okay?"

I sat up. "Yes," my voice barely audible. "Yes, I'm fine. Just taking a bath."

At that moment, I wished he'd enter. We could drain the water and replace it with some that was warmer. He'd slip in next to me, his arms encircling me, and the whirlpool would spin around us. Then he'd rub my back and I'd turn to face him. Softly, slowly, he'd pull me to him, and we'd make love. Kissing, touching, and calling each other's names over soft moans.

"Okay." His voice crashed through my fantasy. "Get out and get some sleep. We have to study our missions. We roll at 1800." That was six p.m. What time was it anyway? "You hungry?" he added, and I wished he'd break down the door and see how hungry I was.

"A little," I admitted.

"Good, chow at 1400 hours. Okay?"

"Fine." Shivering, I pushed out of the tub, grabbed one of the bathrobe-like towels, and buried myself in its fluffiness.

I slipped into a velvet robe hanging on the back of the bathroom door and hugged it around me. Then, washing my face, I spied Estée Lauder creams. It had been over a month since I'd put on any lotion. I felt like a little girl in her mother's makeup as I took handfuls and rubbed my pinked skin from head to toe. After I applied light makeup, I exited out to the room.

Owen stood there. I looked around him to see if Daisy was asleep, but she was gone. My heart kicked up a notch. "Where? What?"

He took my chin into his hand and his lips found mine.

I pulled back. "Where'd Daisy go?"

"Ross demanded to change rooms and, well, I wanted to see you." His fingers felt warm as he slipped the robe from my shoulders, and it fell to the floor at my feet. His hands played with the skin on my arms and traveled downward to my fingers. He lifted my hands to encircle his neck and yanked my hips toward him. I gasped air and chewed on my lower lip, wanting more than anything for him to take me.

Wait a minute. Why was he here? It took every ounce of willpower for me to wrench back. "Is this why you brought me? For recreation? You don't speak to me for a week, and then you enter my room, uninvited, to force yourself on me?"

He pulled back. "Force myself on you? Recreation? I'm sorry." He picked up the jacket he must have dropped on the floor. "You're right. This was a mistake. I won't bother you again."

Panic seized me. No matter what the reason he came, he was there. "No. Don't go." I clasped his shoulders. Pressing him backward, we fell onto the bed. "Please don't ever go." I kissed him, and he maneuvered us the rest of the way onto the mattress.

On all fours, I groped for his jeans. I wanted Owen to love me. To tell me as much. I wanted to belong with him. Feel that deep connection. In no time, he was inside of me, and I was rocking over him, filled with the feeling of him deep between my thighs. Inviting him in so he was filling me. Wanting to be one with him.

Minutes later, spent, I dropped to lay beside him. I rested my hand on his heaving chest. He sat up, leaned over, and kissed my forehead. "You have to get some sleep. I'll go."

"No, stay." Had my words sounded so desperate?

He smiled and pulled the comforter over me. His hand grazed my cheek. "Sleep, baby." Then he bent and tenderly kissed my lip before turning to the door. I grabbed onto his hand. I bit back the urge to tell him how much I loved him, afraid I'd scare him away. Wanting him to stay, I released him.

As the door fell back and his footfalls quieted, thoughts of frustration attacked me. I was so weak. No wonder he could come and go as he pleased. I made it so easy for the robot of a man to use me. These thoughts collided with my fantasies of us together every night. I pounded my pillow. Sleep was out.

I didn't realize I had dozed until I woke to a pounding on the door. "Chow," Daisy said through the wood, and I heard her retreat. Owen? Then I remembered he'd left. My cheeks flushed. What if Daisy had heard us? I rolled my eyes; that wouldn't keep me from him.

I slipped back into my jeans and went down to the ballroom-sized dining room. I avoided looking into his eyes as I pushed into a velvet cushion oak chair next to George. "Some digs," he said.

"Where's our host?" I whispered to George.

"Our host can't be seen with us." Owen emphasized the word "host" letting me know he'd heard me. "He and his family are at Martha's Vineyard for the weekend." Owen's smile made my stomach tickle.

A maid in a white apron entered and placed two large porcelain bowls of steaming soup on the table. A butler entered with bread. I clutched the water goblet and squeezed a lemon wedge into mine.

"I told the help we'd serve ourselves," Owen said as the maid and butler disappeared.

George dribbled tomato soup on the lace tablecloth, but otherwise we handled ourselves pretty well for government issue.

The soft homemade bread melted on my tongue, and the salmon was so fresh I thought it might have been caught that day right out of the lake behind the house. The freshness of the beef, however, I didn't speculate. I ate until my stomach hurt. But I consumed the entire wedge of seven-layer chocolate cake anyway, along with a healthy spoonful of vanilla bean ice cream.

As soon as the dishes were carted away, Owen went over every detail of the plan again, quizzing us on our parts.

THE MISSION

By 1800 we rolled out. The short brown wig I wore made my head itch. Owen wore a suit with a long blond hair-piece that made him look like a surfer boy. His sunglasses hid his eyes and looked out of place in the darkness of the evening. He also had a fake mustache. Harry, whose real name was Smith, had a red beard.

Owen dropped George and me at the parking structure where two employees raised eyebrows in our direction. Owen exited the limo and gave them one hundred dollars each to reserve the fourth floor for our party. He explained that George and I were to stay up on the fourth to keep guard. For an additional hundred, the men agreed to keep their boss out of it. Then we waited.

I turned on the phone and read the time, 1820. Across the street, red and green lights blinked in the window of a pizzeria. The bookstore next to it had a Santa painted on the window with his nose in a book. I squinted to make out the book's title, Fifty Shades of Grey. Seriously, who would perverse the image of Santa Claus?

Next to me, George looked out at the sign too. "What are you thinking?" he asked.

I smiled at him. "This is crazy, right?"

He sighed. "I don't want to think too hard about it." His lips pressed together, and then in a whisper he added, "But maybe it's the time of year." I wondered what to say to that, but before I could say anything he continued, "Sometimes I wonder about home."

Home. A moment of guilt seized me. None of us had a home anymore. My mom and stepfather thought I was in rehab in Mexico. Did George have parents who would miss him at Christmas? For that matter, did he have a wife, maybe kids? How do you make a life just disappear? Yes, I'd wondered about Owen. I'd wanted to know where he was from. Who he'd loved and if that love affected me.

"Are you married?" I asked.

He got a faraway look in his eyes as if a memory was packed away somewhere under layers of the kids he'd felt responsible for killing with poisoned drugs. And under more layers of training and a promise of making a difference in this world. But not forgotten, not completely.

"Divorced."

"Sorry."

"She left me." He picked at a cuticle, and I noticed his nails were bitten down to the quick. All were raw and red. "Didn't have the stamina for all the court shit." He blinked back moisture that collected at the bottom lid of his eyes. His voice was raspy when he added, "Two years of sheer hell, and she got to cash out of it."

I resisted the urge to reach out and touch his arm. As a nurse in Bagram, I'd uselessly comforted people who had lost a leg to an IED, soldiers who'd been shot. I knew a touch couldn't erase any of that, but did it say "You're not alone"? Maybe in this case, it said, "Stop, I can't hold up your pain. It's too heavy." When a long minute of silence followed, I repeated, "I'm sorry."

He shrugged. "What are you going to do?"

"Do you regret it?" I asked.

"Regret what?"

"This. All of this?" I spread my hands out to include the parking lot and street below.

"Almost every day."

A bong sounded, making me start. I didn't ask him to elaborate as I lifted my phone in my hand. The text message icon blinked on the cell's face. "Target identified. All players in position. Driver is out and stored in trunk. Nest is ready for target. Copy. We roll in twenty."

My heart raced. My hands shook as I imagined what could go wrong. The creep, Akbar, could have a weapon. That was a real possibility with an arms dealer. He might shoot Owen.

George and I were there because we had medical experience. I gnawed on my lower lip then started on my nails. They were still looking pretty good for the time being.

Another message popped up on my cell. "Target is with an innocent. His daughter. Too late to abort. We roll now."

My breath stuck in my throat. What were they planning? The dealer had his kid with him. Bile hit my stomach. Surely they wouldn't kill a little kid.

I paced over the roof-top parking. George and I had put up traffic cones, and only two other cars were up there. Gravel rolled under my shoes, and puffs of breath escaped my lips. George caught up to me. "Karen, you're pale. Are you okay?" I leaned over the side of the parking structure and vomited.

"You sick?" George sounded miles away through the pulsing in my ears.

I stood up and nodded. "I'm fine. It's just." I had to pause to take a gulp of air. "It's just a kid. Would they kill a kid?"

Minutes later, the limo came charging up the ramp. I froze. Hassan was in the front passenger's seat, and he jumped out first. Owen shoved out next and threw open the back door. "Fisher, Harrison, get over here."

I had to force my feet toward the vehicle. The lights in the back were on, and Smith clutched his shoulder from a position in the back. He held a gun on an Arab man who looked like Hassan.

On the other side of the man sat a tiny bronze-skinned girl wearing a white head scarf with eyes so wide they took up most of her face. "Fisher, get the girl. Harrison, get the first aid kit. We need to patch up Smith. He's been shot."

Trembling, I reached for the girl, who clutched her father. "You son of a bitch," the father yelled. "I will hunt down all of your children and behead them. You've killed everyone close to you."

At that, Owen pistol-slapped him on the side of his face. The girl screamed, and I snatched her up. "Take her down to the first floor," Owen said. He applied a silencer to his Glock.

Akbar grabbed his daughter, and Owen put the Glock to his temple. Akbar let go, but the girl clasped her father's shoulder. I pulled her free and turned to run with the writhing child.

My hands felt slick, and I feared I'd drop her. She hardly weighed a thing, but she twisted and turned so much she was hard to grasp.

She stopped fighting me as I sagged against a pillar on the second parking tier. Dizzy, I felt my heart hammering against my back, and my breath came in pants. Letting my back slide down the pole, I pulled the girl onto my lap.

A man walked by and eyed us like I was strangling the girl. "Are you okay?" he asked, clutching his briefcase closer to him.

"Yes, fine, thank you." I felt the heat in my face and figured I probably looked like I'd wrestled with a bear. "She... she just saw a scary movie." Okay that was convincing. "And... yes, and it was too dark in the upper parking tier, so we're waiting for my husband here."

I searched his eyes to see if he would start dialing 9-1-1. Before he could ask me what movie or the name of my daughter, the squeal of tires caused us both to look toward the ramp going up to the top floor.

Our black SUV sped by me, turned right, and ascended. Daisy was returning to pick everyone up. "Crazy woman driver," I said to the man, as if it made us co-conspirators against the rest of this insane world. He just shook his head and moved off.

Minutes later, the tapping of men's dress shoes resounded off the cold concrete, and Hassan or the arms dealer—I couldn't tell which—approached us. I stiffened. If it was Akbar, he had taken out our entire team. I'd be next. But Hassan's voice said, "Fisher, I can take her from here," and I let out a held breath.

Hassan walked over and whispered to the girl. He took her hand. They turned toward the ramp. I stood up and brushed myself off.

The limo stopped in front of Hassan. I squinted, but it wasn't Owen in the driver's seat. I exchanged a "Who the hell are you" look with Hassan. Then I remembered: Owen said the driver was knocked out in the truck. He ran out and went to the back door.

"Very sorry, sir." His English was excellent. "Don't know what happened. Must have fallen asleep."

"Never mind that," Hassan said. "Just don't let it happen again. Get us home. It is Jasmine's bed-time."

Little Jasmine looked back at me one time and curled her fingers in an abbreviated wave. I thought about Fatima. I wondered if she was dead.

When the limo descended and turned the corner out of sight, I started walking toward the fourth floor. Halfway up the ramp, the SUV swerved to a stop with the side door directly in front of me. I opened it, and the interior light illuminated George and Smith in the front seat. George clasped Smith's shoulder, applying pressure to a sling. Blood seeped through the bandage, and Smith's skin had a powdery white hue. Daisy sat in the driver's seat. I started to slide into the back seat but noticed the black body bag.

Oh God no. "Owen?" I asked.

"Get in. Lover boy's not coming."

"That's not him?"

"No, that's the perp." Daisy floored it before I could close the door all the way.

She stopped by the exit gate. As she gave the overpaid employees a twenty, I said, "Wait. I'll stay with Owen. He may need help."

"No way. Lover boy doesn't need you right now."

"What is that supposed to mean?" I snarled at her.

She pulled out onto the street. "Anybody can see the way you two drool over each other. If you haven't hit that yet, then it's only a matter of time." She laughed an ugly laugh and took a right at the light.

The next hour was a daze of forest and shovel, dumping the body, and getting Smith back to the house where a doctor and scalpel waited. We were supposed to bury our burner phones with the body, but I kept mine. I needed to get hold of Owen.

After scanning the texts for Owen's number, I typed, "Where are you? Are you okay?" Nothing came back.

It was about ten p.m. when we returned to the house. My stomach still hurt, and I went to the bathroom to clean up. I made the water extra warm and soaked under the bubbles. Every few seconds I glanced over the edge of the tub at my burner cell lying silently on the bathmat.

I dressed in a T-shirt and sweatpants and went down into the living room. A fire crackled in the brick fireplace, and Daisy cleaned her .45 at the coffee table. I sat on the couch trying unsuccessfully to keep my gaze from the door.

My eyes darted to the German cuckoo clock on the wall. Eleven p.m., and still no Owen. I took my nail from my mouth where I'd chewed it ragged. Finally, I got up and ran into the bathroom. I threw up again and then put a washcloth to my burning cheeks. Then I called his number.

"Who's this?" His words slurred.

"Owen?"

"No, that's me. Who's this?"

"Where are you? Are you drunk?"

"Don't know," he answered. Then his mouth got farther from the phone. "Hey, you, where am I?"

"Georgetown Pub," I heard in the background.

"In a pub," Owen said. "Where are you?"

"At the house. Come home. We're supposed to be keeping a low profile. Come back now. Don't get in any trouble."

"Trouble." He laughed and then added, "Hit me again, barkeep, and give this lovely lady one too."

Lovely lady? "Owen, get in a cab right now."

"Oh, I can't talk on this phone. They might trace it back to us. Spy stuff." I heard a thud and a crash, and the phone went dead.

I tried the number again, and it rang and rang. Then I dialed information for a cab and gave them my address. I was going to get him.

The cab ride took forty minutes, and the freeway was busy with Friday night traffic. I got out and handed the driver my last forty bucks. I hoped Owen had cash, or we'd have to hit up an ATM on the way home.

Fluorescent lights with beer slogans lit up the window of the otherwise dark brick building. The pink neon u in "Pub" was burned out so the sign read "Georgetown P b."

I pushed in the door to the sound of rock and roll and the swivel of desperate-looking faces. What a hole-in-the-wall. A pool table stood at my right, and the two men holding cubes looked hard ridden and hung up wet. Greasy dark bangs fell into their eyes like dirty curtains.

My pink tee and sweats looked as foreign as if I'd stepped into a bar straight out of Star Wars. Yellow lighting, the smell of old cigarettes, BO, and black leather filled the space from one brick wall to the other. Owen stuck out in his suit. A busty woman draped around him as they pounded shots. I slid into the seat next to him.

"Hey." His wet eyes shone with recognition. His woman friend looked me up and down and adjusted the strap on her brassiere, making her abundant bosom lift a few inches. "What are you doing here, Fisher?"

"Name's Cathy," I said, trying to remind him not to blow our covers. I forgot his fake name. I'd been too preoccupied lately to remember details. Maybe I needed a vacation.

I linked my arm in his and whispered close to his ear. "We have to get out of here, Owen. Come on. Come back with me. The meter in the cab is still running ."

At that, the hooker on his other side piped up. "Look, honey, go find your own date for tonight. This one is spoken for." Between her yellow teeth, her breath reeked of nicotine.

"Look, miss, my husband and I are leaving here."

"You never told me you was married." She rubbed her nose like a meth head. "You had me wasting my time on you. You promised me a date."

"I'm not leaving." Owen's voice was loud over the music. "I'm sitting here and having a drink."

"Looks like you've had enough," I said. I bent close to his ear again and whispered. "Come on, Owen, we can't be out here like this. It could blow the whole operation."

"I don't give a shit." He shrugged me off. Then he looked at me like he was recognizing me for the first time. "Okay. We can go but I'm not going back to the house, not right now."

"Fine. We can go anywhere you want to."

"I don't know." He rubbed his face. "I'm so tired."

"Let's get out of here. Maybe go get some coffee at Denny's or somewhere. We'll talk, okay?"

"Did you see her?"

"Who?" I looked at the prostitute who had her skirt hiked up to her waist and had moved over next to the pool players. She appeared to be pulling up the holey nylons and picking at her crotch at the same time. I squirmed in the vinyl chair, hoping I won't catch something.

Owen touched my shoulder. "The little girl. Did you see her?"

"Kafferdy, we can't talk about that here. Let's talk about it somewhere else."

"No, I don't want to talk about her." He turned to the bartender. "Give me another. And give Fisher one too." He looked back at me. "What are you drinking, doll?"

"My name's Cathy." I smiled into the rugged face of the bartender. "AA." I added then to Owen, "I can't drink, remember? I can't do it without getting drunk, and one of us has to stay sober. I can't be here. Please take me somewhere else."

"Okay." He got up and stumbled so the bar stool wobbled like it would fall over. I grabbed the chair as he placed a fifty on the bar. He almost left his wallet too but I grabbed it. I handed it to him as we made for the door. He put his arm around my shoulder, and we staggered onto the cobble-stone street.

I couldn't let the team see him like that. And I was exhausted from our trip and had little sleep. In California it was only nine p.m., but I needed to go somewhere I could sit down. I longed to take off my shoes and sober Owen up before we headed back to Silver Spring.

I pointed to the Renaissance Hotel around the corner. "Let go check into that hotel for the night."

"You want to take advantage of me, doll," he said, breathing fumes into my face.

"My dream date," I said and had to hold him back from crossing the street against the light.

We gave Owen's credit card to the bleary-eyed young man at the counter, and I clutched the key to room 105 until we were safely inside. While I double-bolted the door, Owen opened the mini bar. "Whoa, I think you've had enough," I said, reaching for the can of Miller in his hand.

"No, the night is still young. Unless you want to play. You want to play, doll. That's why you came to get me. I'm all yours." He fell backward on to the bed, and I noted the comforter was the cheap rayon kind that snags and itches. I sighed. I had so looked forward to sleeping on the 800-count Egyptian cotton back at the house.

Then Owen sat up. "Karen, did you see the girl? Did you see her?" And suddenly I knew the girl he was talking about.

"Yes. She's okay, Owen. She's with Hassan."

"He said he'd find my daughter and behead her. He'd find my daughter. I put her in danger. Doing this I put her in danger. I can't do that, Karen. I can't hurt everyone I touch." Water filled his eyes as he bowed his head.

I sat down and took his head in my hands. I ran my fingers through his hair, short again without the surfer-boy hair piece. "It's okay. He's dead. We buried him."

I pushed down the bile I felt rising in my throat at the thought of watching that body bag drop into the hole. I pictured Daisy and George digging, all the while complaining that I got the easy job of applying pressure to Smith's shoulder wound. Like getting blood all over me as it seeped through the bandages was a piece of cake. Or being petrified that he'd die from the blood loss was a walk in the park.

"He shot Smith," Owen said as if reading my thoughts. "I couldn't protect him. I didn't know he'd have the girl with him. I don't like hurting kids."

"You didn't hurt her." I continued to rub his head as he shed tears on my shoulder. His arms clutched me tightly. "She's fine," I bend my head to whisper in his ear. "She's fine because of you."

"I've got to make sure she's okay."

"Just call Hassan. He'll tell you. He's there with her now."

"No, she's with her mother and that man she married. He adopted her. She doesn't have my name anymore."

Then it dawned on me, he was talking about his own daughter. "How old is she?" I asked. He shook his head without lifting it from my shoulder. "Do you know where she lives? Maybe you could write her. Send a card. Let her know you're thinking of her."

He lifted his head and tapped a finger to his temple. "I know. She's in Fairfax, Virginia. He might be able to get to her."

"Are you talking about Jasmine or your daughter?"

"Susie. She lives in Fairfax, 157 Kings Court. She lives in Fairfax... " With that he rolled away from me and dropped to the mattress. When I leaned over him, I saw his eyes were closed.

I watched him drool on the sheet until was sure I wouldn't wake him if I moved. Then I gently pulled the comforter and sheets down and slipped into the bed beside him.

Light seeped between the gauzy curtains, and a sheer ring sounded from my phone. I bolted upright and looked over at Owen's still profile. The acidic sting of nausea from the night before filled my stomach, and my head throbbed from the erratic sleep. I reached down and snatched up the phone.

"Fisher?" came the voice of Young.

"Yes."

"Where are you?"

"I'm with Owen. We're at Denny's." I stood and distanced myself from Owen in case he gave my lie away.

"The team is worried about you, and the phone is being traced." So much for hiding it. If they were tracing the call, they'd know we were in a hotel. "Why didn't you burn it as instructed?"

"I had to go find Owen."

"Burn it now and use a public phone to notify the team that you haven't been captured." Then the line went dead.

I reached into the mini fridge to get a Hersey bar with almonds to settle my stomach and hopefully ease my headache. Then I took the battery from the phone and, with the aid of the lamp, smashed the body of the phone. At the end table, I spotted the phone book. Where was Fairfax, Virginia, anyway?

I glanced at the bottles of wine and beer in the mini fridge and decided I didn't need them. I could be strong for Owen now. I left the room to get a map of Virginia from the lobby and borrowed a computer to look up the directions to 157 Kings Court in Fairfax. The house was only nineteen miles away.

WHO IS OWEN?

I printed the instructions and charged the cost to the room under Owen's credit card. Glancing at the clock, I noticed the time was nine a.m. We could go to Virginia and get back in time to make the flight back to California.

Owen hadn't stirred in my absence, and I made a pot of strong coffee from the complimentary stuff in the room. After taking a quick shower, I nudged his shoulder. "Owen. Come on. We have to go now."

His bloodshot eyes opened one and at time. He looked at me without recognition until I handed him one of the paper cups and sat down on the side of the bed. As he sat up, I called a cab and went down to the lobby with his wallet to settle the bill.

With mussed hair, Owen stumbled out of the room wearing his sunglasses.

I got into the cab first. He ducked to get in as well only to bang his head on the cab's doorframe. We took off. He didn't question where until we were a mile from our destination. Then he bolted up in the seat and looked out the window. "Where are we, Fisher?"

"Fairfax."

"What? Why?"

"You need to see her. Make sure she's okay. Then we'll go."

"No," he said. "I can't. I can't ever be part of her life again. It's too dangerous."

The cab made a smooth turn to the left and Owen said, "No. Take us to Silver Springs. Now."

The cabby looked back at us through the rearview mirror. "The lady said 157 King's Court. We're here, sir." He stopped in front of the house.

The lawn was green, and there was a tree in the front. Beyond that was a large window looking into a breakfast nook. A girl with golden blond hair sat at the table. She must have been five or six. She dipped a spoon into a bowl.

Owen didn't answer the driver but fixed his eyes on that window. "Sir, do you want to get out or should we leave?"

"Give us a minute," I said. I touched Owen's shoulder, and he looked back at me. "Do you want to get out?"

He shook his head. "No, Fisher." Then he looked back toward the house. His lip buckled as he said, "She's gotten so big." He tore his eyes from the scene. "We can go."

A woman with short blond hair and a belly that was extended with pregnancy walked behind the chair of the child. She stopped and squinted out at the cab for what felt like a frozen minute before she disappeared.

Was that her? Was that Owen's wife? The door flung open, and she waddled toward the car. Through the window, a tall, dark-haired man held the little girl's hand as they both peered out at the cab and the woman.

The driver started to pull away from the curb, but I protested. "No. Wait."

Owen's mouth hung open, and I reached across the seat to open the door. He clutched it so it wouldn't swing open. "Go. Talk to her. She knows you're here," I said, even though a part of me wanted him to slam the door and tell me he didn't want to see her.

He let the door swing open and got out. The woman glared at him. Her mouth pressed in a tight line. Then she yelled, "What the hell are you—you can't just show up like this!" He took it all with his head bowed.

Then the woman seemed to crumble. "She doesn't know you. She's happy."

Owen nodded. "Okay." He reached in his wallet and produced a wad of bills. "Give her something. Anything she needs."

The woman hit the bills from his hand. "Is that what this is about? Relieving your guilt with money? Go away, Michael, and don't come back here." Had I heard her right? Had she said "Michael"?

"I'm sorry. I just… "

"Just what?"

"Nothing."

"What, Michael? You wanted to see us? Well, you have. Now goodbye."

There it was again. Could Michael be his middle name? A pet name, just between the two of them, and one thing was clear—she still loved him. I was sure of it, but how did he feel? He held out a hand. "Congratulations on the baby."

Then the woman seemed to notice me. She charged toward the cab. "Are you? Are you with him?"

I recoiled a little in the seat. "We're just... "

Owen had her by the shoulders. "I'm leaving, Brenda. I won't bother you again."

"He'll leave you too, you know. He'll leave you too. It's what he does best." The woman wiped tears from her cheeks.

I noticed her husband was at the door. "Brenda, you okay?"

"It's okay, Sam. He's just leaving."

Then the little girl broke from the man's hand and ran across the lawn. She threw herself into her mother's hip. "Mommy. Why are you crying, Mommy?"

Owen bent to the child. The little girl recoiled from him. She was almost behind her mother.

Owen reached a hand out to his daughter. "Hi, my name is Michael," he said.

The little girl stared at the hand but didn't take it. A second later she glanced at her mom. "Who is he, Mommy? Who is he?"

The husband materialized and scooped the girl up in his arms. "Let's go back in the house, Susie."

Owen remained kneeling as the family turned to leave. Sam put a hand on Brenda's shoulder. She turned to look at Owen one more time before she let her husband lead her away.

Owen's lips buckled as he headed back to the car and got in. He said nothing, and I didn't know whether to reach out to him or not. With his arms crossed he was blocking me out of his world. This wasn't my world anyway.

"Let's go," I whispered to the driver, regretting my decision to come in the first place. "Unless you want to stop somewhere else first?"

Owen shook his head. On the pretense of rubbing his eyes, he discreetly swiped at tears that slipped past the lens of his sunglasses. I politely pretended not to notice, all the while my heart was breaking. We drove in silence the rest of the way to the house.

The team piled suitcases into the black SUV when we pulled into the circular drive. "Where you been?" Daisy asked, and then with a sneer, added, "No time for a bootie call when we got to get out of here."

Owen didn't respond, but I told her to shut up. I noticed my suitcase was already packed and sat next to the SUV. I put it in, wishing I could go back to that Jacuzzi tub and wash the past twenty-four hours away.

On the plane home, I stole a multitude of glances toward Owen. He looked out the window and never returned my gaze.

Damn it anyway. I'd only tried to help. Trying to save the world shouldn't come at such a high price. Then I thought of the novels East of Eden, The Thorn Birds, A Tale of Two Cities—the books that had made me want to study English. No, life wasn't fair, but at least we had a choice. I wanted a family, kids who loved me, and a man who stuck by my side. I knew Owen wanted that too. I just needed to convince him that it was possible.

Okay, I know, we'd just killed a father who was bent on making the world the way he wanted it, and we'd endangered his daughter, but Owen wasn't Akbar. Then it occurred to me: did Hassan have a family he left behind? In the story I'd made up about Hassan, he had a family, maybe two sons and two daughters. And somehow that was not enough for him. He risked it all because he was consumed with his feelings that babies were being slaughtered at clinics and he needed to stop it with a bomb.

Department G took advantage of the situation and made a deal: no jail for the bombing, but a life away from his family all the same. Or maybe not a life, but ten or fifteen years. Then what? He'd desert one family to go back to his original one. Or would he have forged a new life with Jasmine and her mother? Maybe they'd even have more kids, and he'd be unable to leave it. He'd need to see his kids through their childhoods—need to be at Jasmine's graduation. Why couldn't we all live two lives? Why couldn't there be a happy ending?

HOME AGAIN

Owen didn't talk to me when we got back to base. Two new trainees had joined the team. One was Arab, and I didn't trust his too-close-set eyes and tight, angry little mouth. But I hadn't trusted Hassan either, and he'd been a loyal member of Department G. The second trainee was French, and they sat together at all times.

George sat down next to me in the cafeteria as I stifled a yawn. "What, your social life getting in the way of your beauty sleep, or are you just bored with me?"

I glared at him. For the last few nights, I'd had a disturbing dream. Aidan stood in front of me with a gun. Fear froze in my veins. He turned and shot at students who bobbed up and down like in a carnival game. Alice's face exploded. I yelled, "Stop! Please stop!"

He turned to me, smirking. Then he passed the butt of the gun to me. I shook my head at it. "No. Put it away," I whispered. He wordlessly pushed the gun toward me again. But my arms had disappeared. I couldn't take it even if I wanted to.

He laughed and said, "You can't do your own dirty work, can you? No, someone else has to torture me." He tried giving me the gun again, and it transformed into a snake. The snake's forked tongue struck him in the face. Then it wrapped around his neck so his eyes bulged, and he whispered, "You couldn't do it yourself."

I wanted to tell George about the dream, but I was too embarrassed.

Owen, of course, had been AWOL, so I couldn't ask him about Aidan or tell him of my dream. I was surprised when two days passed and Owen finally appeared at my shoulder during chow. "Fisher, I need you to work tonight."

I looked up at him. "Doing what?" I asked. I'd seen little of him at PT or self-defense. Probably avoiding me or—my mind flashed back to Aidan—was he too busy torturing him?

"Cleaning the lab on the third floor? We have a guest, and we need the kitchen cleaned and bio-waste discarded."

"Guest"—is that what we were calling a prisoner? "Third floor," I repeated. I sat up and pointed to the office I'd eavesdropped outside before we left for DC. So an opportunity to see what condition Aidan was in had dropped into my lap.

"Yep. Shouldn't take more than a few hours. Right after evening chow."

"Sure." How easy was that? Wait, I might not be allowed in there alone. Perhaps they'd have a guard watching me, or Owen would accompany me. Something about the nightmare made me want to be alone. Aidan had told me I couldn't do my own dirty work. I was killing him, but not with a gun and not as a conscious choice. No, I was not brave enough for that. He was right about me. But being alone in the same room as him—that idea both excited and frightened me. "I'm finished. Should I just go up there now?"

"Sure. Here's the key, and the supplies are in there. Our guest is in the back room sleeping, so don't bother him."

"I'll go with," George said. "I need to monitor his vitals since he was given his last dose of Zap."

Darn, not alone. Followed, of course. Then I let what he'd said sink in. "Zap? What's that?" I asked.

George's smile broadened. "I developed it. It's part Ecstasy and tryptophan. Along with some opiates and a few other drugs. To make a cocktail that—"

"Enough chitchat." Owen cut him off. "Just get moving if you're going, and Harrison, I need to talk to you. You can follow Fisher later."

Chewing on my healing bottom lip, I blurted, "I was a nurse. Maybe I could just check the vitals myself." In Afghanistan I'd dealt with a few drug overdoses that I suspected were suicide attempts. Opium was involved in one case, and the user had had horrible violent hallucinations.

"No." Owen's voice was hard. "I mean, just let him sleep. Harrison can check on him." I could get more warmth out of a stone.

I probed my lip where Aidan had split it a week earlier. I wondered if Owen remembered Aidan attacking me. Maybe he was being gallant. Wanting to safeguard me. Dream on. More likely he didn't trust me—felt I screwed everything up, even his smooth separation from his daughter.

I moved to the stairs and looked over my shoulder at the boys. Owen spoke close to George's face. George's eyes widened, he shoved his hands deep into the pockets of his jeans, then he looked at the floor, shaking his head. Owen nodded and turned, almost catching me staring before I pivoted and marched up the steps.

George caught up with me before I opened the door to the room. "I didn't know you were a nurse. I was a medic in the Army. It's where I got my first taste of pharmaceuticals."

I placed the key in the lock as he continued. "I thought you said you were a teacher."

"Yep. I was a nurse a long time ago. Water under the bridge," I said. "I can still take vitals and do first aid, but I'm afraid I've let my CPR certification expire. So, what's wrong with that man, Aidan, anyway?" I pushed open the door and was assaulted with an antiseptic smell.

George gulped a few times, avoiding my eyes. "We're just keeping him sedated so he doesn't get too upset."

"With Ecstasy?" I asked.

"Karen, you know I'm not supposed to talk about my work. We each have our jobs to do, and Kafferdy asked me to remind you to clean the bathroom. The supplies are all in the cabinet."

"Yeah. Thanks," I said.

The next hour I spent cleaning the bathrooms and mopping the floor. There was some blood on the bathroom floor, and I wondered if Aidan had cut himself. There were also three metal bedpans soaking in the bathtub. Had they hurt Aidan so badly that he couldn't get up to use the toilet?

I took my time cleaning, and George finally decided he had to get back to his duties on the first floor. It was my opportunity to get to Aidan and see what I could do. I pushed through the door next to the bathroom to find him shackled to the hospital bed.

I leaned over the bed and heard him exhale. The IV needle was still inserted in the back of his hand. His breathing was shallow and rapid. He jerked every so often. His dirty, matted hair clung to his scalp, and he'd grown a beard. His cheek sported scratch marks. I touched his wrist to feel his pulse. It was faster than I expected. "What did I do to you? What did I allow them to do to you?" I whispered. I touched the straps that held down his arms and noticed more scratch marks. He'd been tearing at his skin. The metal of the buckle bit into his hand. Okay, I can do this. Give him a chance to escape. When Owen found out, would he think someone had forgotten to secure the strap?

"Fisher," I heard behind me, and my heart slammed against my ribs at Owen's voice. "What are you doing?"

"I... I... why are you drugging him? He's torn his skin, and his face is gaunt with lost weight. He isn't his brother, Owen. We can't just torture him because of who his brother is."

Owen strode across the room and stood beside me. His hand covered mine, still posed over the buckle. He lifted it in his and tightened his grip. "He's not innocent. He attacked you."

"So let him face charges in court. Not this vigilante justice." I reached down and, pulling against Owen's grip, fingered the buckle.

"You can't save the world, Fisher. When are you going to get that through your head? Some things come with a price. You can't keep living in your Cinderella and Sleeping Beauty world."

"So that's it. I'm sorry I wanted you to see your daughter, Owen. You were worried about her. I made a judgment call, but you put that alcohol to your lips before I got there, remember? You want to pretend you don't feel, but you do. You're human, Owen, and you do."

"God damn it, Karen. I can't afford to feel." His hands shook as he clasped my wrist. "Don't you see I'm doing this for them, for all of us? If I make this world better, it's for all of us."

"So let him go. We can do it another way. Think of what Fatima is doing, or has already done?"

"You don't understand, Karen. We need him not only to take out his brother, but we have a deal in place."

"Are you ransoming him off?" Surely his brother wouldn't take his place.

"No. They have Fatima."

I released the buckle. "Fatima. What happened?"

"Someone discovered her before she could get to her target. They kidnapped her. We hear she's still alive, but we don't know for how long. We relayed a message to Aidan's brother Marcus, and he is willing to trade his brother for her."

"So you're torturing him to get even for Fatima?

"No, we're training him to take out Marcus."

I tried to snatch my hand back, but Owen held fast. "He's going to kill his own brother?" I asked.

"Think of the alternatives." He pressed my hand to his chest, and I noticed its rapid rhythm. "We send in a drone and maybe take out Marcus and the others, plus God knows what else. But this way, this dirtbag gets to be a hero. Save lives."

I swallowed the lump in my throat and stepped in closer toward Owen so my chin was against his sternum. "I know something about being considered a hero. You have to live with the aftermath. He kills his brother, and he has to live with that."

Owen's hands dropped to my hip where he pushed me a few inches from him, still clutching the skin over my pelvis bones. "That's much better than allowing his brother to keep killing innocent people. What would you have done to save your students?"

"That's not fair." I twisted in an attempt to move away from him.

He grabbed my waist pulling me completely into him as I attempted to turn away. "Would you have shot Rodney Jasper? Would you have taken his life, if it would have saved your students? If you could have sacrificed his life for theirs ?"

My breaths were coming rapidly now, and I felt panicky. "That's up to the courts to decide."

"There are no international courts to stop these guys, Karen. So I'm asking, would you have shot Rodney Jasper to stop him from shooting everyone at your school?"

I looked at the floor and he put his hand on my chin lifting it. "Yes," I said. "Yes. I would have." Maybe Owen was right. How many times did I hear about a criminal getting off due to a technicality? A smoking gun thrown out of court because the cops didn't have a proper warrant, but it was still the weapon that killed the victim? But the courts seemed more interested in protecting the criminals. Maybe Department G was getting it right. "Why are you torturing him, though? Isn't there a better way?"

Owen sighed. "God, sometimes around you I feel weak." And suddenly my stomach felt like it melted. I wanted to envelope him in my arms; somehow, maybe together we'd be strong. But as I reached around his waist, he grabbed my arms back. He continued, "We're not torturing him. Harrison has come up with a drug that helps us program him."

God help me, all I wanted to do was throw myself at this man and let him protect me from the world, but at the same time I wanted him to see that he didn't need to be that guy who stayed on the ugly side of humanity. He didn't need to constantly deal with death and destruction, because that was a place I couldn't live with him. So I pushed away from him. "Program him? How will he kill his brother?"

"Cyanide capsule. It will be almost painless. Better than that bastard deserves."

Looking into Owen's face, my eyes filled. "Okay," I said. And I knew I trusted him, believed in what he was doing.

He bent to me and kissed me on the lips. When he pulled away, he said, "I'm glad you understand. I'm glad we're on the same page."

I wrapped my arms around him and pulled him against me. I needed to believe in him. I needed to feel him protecting me. And in his arms, everything was okay again.

Owen clutched my hips and lifted me up so my legs wrapped around his waist. He carried me out of the room. Lowering me to the couch, his hands were a flurry of frenzied motion as he tore at the buttons of my shirt. He pulled his shirt over his head and stepped out of his jeans. When he'd stripped my shirt, he worked on my jeans. He lowered himself to me. His lips kissed at my neck. He slowly worked his way down my side, and after he found his way between my thighs, he lay on top of me. He took my breath away as he entered me. I arched and groaned. "Are you okay?" he asked.

I took a shuddering breath and nodded my head. I curved my back into him. Clinging to him, I pushed worry and doubt away. "I love you." I couldn't stop the words as they escaped from my lips. Owen stopped rocking on top of me.

"God, Karen. What are you doing to me?" Then he seemed to pick up the pace and plunge deeper. His breath came in pants. "I need you."

"Karen," came in a higher-pitched voice from too far away. Not Owen's. I heard the squeak of the door. Owen bolted up in a flash. I looked to the door and saw George's head as I pressed my ruined shirt into my chest. "Oh." George averted his eyes before retreating back out the door. "Sorry, I... "

The door closed again as Owen went for it. He opened it cursing. "Shit, shit, shit." Then he must have noticed he was naked because he didn't charge after George. Instead, he pivoted and returned to my side. "Fuck. I'm an idiot." He slapped his palm against his forehead.

I reached for him, gripping his arm. He pushed me off. "No. I told you we can't do this. I can't let you keep getting under my skin." He didn't look at me.

His words slapped me. I'd told him I loved him. He said he needed me.

He was dressed in a minute. I thought he'd exit without acknowledging me, but at the door, he paused. His shoulders rose and then fell and he took an audible breath. "I'm sorry," he whispered shaking his head before he disappeared.

My lips buckled before the tears came heavy and silently. I rose and got dressed. So that was it. I'd chosen a life that meant never getting close to anyone. Then I stepped down and felt the crunch of dog tags under my feet. My first thought was to run after Owen to return them. No, screw him. Let him come to me.

BRAVE

That night I tossed and turned on my mattress. Owen hadn't come to ask for his keys, and I hadn't seen him at dinner. What a coward. Avoiding me. He might be a big bad terrorist hunter, but he was running from his own feelings. I must have drifted off to sleep because I woke to a voice muttering. I bolted upright in my bed and listened. Cursing and thick-tongued words, "Move it." Then some words in Arabic.

Fear choked me, and I shoved it down. Even if I wanted to hide, I was completely exposed in the room. I slid from my cot and gripped Owen's dog tags. On my hands and knees, I edged toward the side of the room and slowly crawled forward.

Peering out the bars, I saw them: two men. One was the Arab trainee; the other was a man I'd never seen. Between them, Aidan slumped. They started to descend the stairs so that Aidan's head bobbed up and down with each step. I recoiled. Afraid they'd see me, I pressed my back to the wall. That's when I saw him. Owen lay on the ground floor, his face pressed into the tile.

Oh my God. Had they killed him? They were taking Aidan. They could leave, letting others know where we were. Maybe they'd bomb the building, get rid of Department G. The metal of Owen's office key cut into my hand. I tried to ignore it. I wanted to hide like I had done that day. But no, I was the only one around to help Owen. And I knew he kept his Glock in his office.

I looked down at my white tee. No good. I grabbed a black sweatshirt and crawled to the door. The man looked down as they lugged Aidan between them. They stumbled and swore. I slipped out of the room. My whole body shook as I crept toward the far flight of steps.

Then I scooted down them on my butt, keeping low. I held my breath as I got to the bottom. The men didn't notice me as they leaned over a table in the mess. Any minute they could turn around and catch me. I ducked into the kitchen. It was blocked off by a floating wall that covered about ten feet of area. Crouching under the metal shelving, I hustled to the other side. It was only feet from the outer door to the offices where Owen's room was.

Peering around the edge of the floating wall, I noticed they stood near the outer door. They muttered in Arabic. Then the trainee pointed at Owen. "What should we do with him?"

The man I didn't know said, "You go pull up the van. We take him with us."

"What about the files?" Trainee said.

"I'll get them. Do you know where the key is?"

"I've seen them on that chain he wears attached to his neck."

"You go. I'll search him."

At that, Trainee took off, leaving Aidan slumped against the wall. Leader man—I called him Farid—turned Owen over. I had to distract him. But how?

I scanned the serving trays. Okay, metal. I'd throw it. That might wake up someone else, too. It would also alert him that I was there. My heart raced. I could crawl under the metal shelving and hide. Or I could try my best to stop them. I thought of Fatima risking her life—a suicide bomber. Sticking out my chin, I decided I would do this for them. Those I was too weak and scared to fight for. I would do this for my students.

With hands as stable as a landslide I grabbed ladles and some serving spoons on two metal trays. I sucked in a breath as they clattered on the tray. Farid didn't speak, so I guessed he hadn't heard me. Then I snuck to the other side of the kitchen to draw Farid away from the office door.

Taking a shuddering breath, I knew that it was now or never, and I threw them. The clatter on the floor made me wish I had hidden. I ran to the other side and, shivering, peered out. Farid had jumped up. He extended the pistol in his hand. "Who's there?" He looked toward the noise and rose to go away from my side of the room. I waited until he disappeared before I orchestrated the second phase of my plan to distract.

I had three serving spoons left. I added a few knives to my pockets for extra security. I heaved spoons at the glass window toward the back of the cafeteria. The clash and sound of breaking glass reverberated off the walls. I had called Farid to the kitchen for sure.

Shivering, I stood in the doorframe, hoping Farid would come in the far opening to the floating wall so I could slip out the other side and go toward the office. I'd only have seconds to get to the door, unlock it, and go for the gun. And he already had a gun. "Come out from there. I have a weapon," he said, and I heard him step through the opening. I didn't need that reminder twice, and I dashed toward the door.

My sweaty palm slipped from the handle, and I turned the knob. Locked. Owen's dog tags danced in my hand. Behind me, around the bend behind the floating wall, I heard Farid crashing around.

"Come out now or I'll shoot you." He hadn't noticed me yet.

The key slid in the lock. I turned it. The door squealed open. A muted ping of a silenced bullet from behind me made me freeze. Oh God, he was coming. I glanced over my shoulder. He charged forward. "Stop there."

With every ounce of courage I could muster, I slipped my hand into my pocket for a knife. I hurled it at him and, ducking, pushed inside. My hands were like feathers as I groped for the lock. It slid in place. Two muted pings sounded on the door, but it held. Bulletproof.

I could stay there and avoid the gunman, but Owen needed me. I ran to his office, opened the door, and closed it behind me. My ears stayed alert for anything, but all was quiet.

The Glock. I rushed to the drawers, throwing each open to find the gun. I got to the bottom drawer. There it was.

Six bullets in the chamber. I clicked the safety off. It jerked in my hand. Steady, steady. I needed to go back out there.

My feet felt heavy walking back out that door. This time there was no 9-1-1 to dial. No backup plan. Where was everyone else? Why did I have to face this alone? Fear gripped my stomach, and I felt like throwing up.

I got out the door and gritted my teeth as I pushed open the lock. He was out there, ready to shoot me. I slid my back to the far wall and eased the door open. Thrusting the gun out first, I peered around. He wasn't there. I slid from the safety of the wall. Forcing myself to take a breath, I pushed out and held the gun at eye level.

Farid stood over Owen, but he looked up at my approach. Then he laughed. "What do you intend to do with that?"

The Glock shook in my hand. My palm felt slick. Then I surprised myself and pulled the trigger, aiming for his chest. He jerked back and fell, and his gun shot upward. I ducked. I'd hit him. I'd shot him. Light flooded the room.

As in a dream, my feet carried me to Owen. Kneeling, I felt his head. There was a cut on the back of it where they must have knocked him out. I reached for his neck while holding the gun pointed at the door ready for the trainee to return.

Smith yelled behind me. "Fisher, what are you doing?"

"It's them," my voice was all air. I coughed and tried again. "They knocked Owen out. There's one more." It was as if someone brave took over my body. I felt Owen's pulse. Yes, he was alive.

The front door opened, and the trainee entered. I shot again. This time the bullet ricocheted off the wall next to the door. The trainee slammed it shut.

My eyes fell on Farid. His mouth and eyes were open, and his shirt was a mass of blood and tissue. I'd killed a man. The image of the Afghan insurgent in the hospital flooded me. I'd barely been able to hook up his IV. He was all bones and burns. That's when I turned my head to vomit.

Smith was at my side, grabbing the gun from me. Then he turned and took off out the front door. I sat down as the room spun around me. I'd killed a man. I knew it was in self-defense, but dead was dead.

Suddenly, everyone emerged, blinking at the light. Daisy looked down at me, her face a question mark. Then she picked up Farid's gun. Aidan had risen, and George restrained him. I watched as everything seemed to unfold in slow motion. Smith dragged Trainee's body back into the room. The French trainee and Daisy got body bags to put the bodies in.

Daisy passed me and said, "You shoot him?"

I nodded and she bobbed her head back in approval. Then I remembered Owen. I called for a first aid kit and cradled his head in my lap. I used gauze to wrap his head, and his eyes blinked open. "Fisher," he said.

"It's alright. We got them."

Smith came to walk Owen back to his room, and I went for a mop to clean the floor. Then it hit me. For the first time in a long time, I didn't need a drink.

It was two hours later when Smith came to tell us Owen was going to be alright. I went back to bed but couldn't sleep.

I finally got up and went down to Owen's office. Smith was sleeping in the chair next to him when I entered. "Fisher, what are you...?"

I flashed him the dog tags. "Returning these. I'll sit with him. I can't sleep."

Smith rose and left without another word. I looked down at Owen. He looked pale. I had advised Smith to wake him every hour to make sure he hadn't passed out from a massive brain hemorrhage. I tapped his shoulder, and his eyes popped open.

"Thought you'd need these." I dangled them before his face as I leaned over the couch he used as a bed.

"Karen, Fisher... What happened?"

I told him all I knew. That two men had tried to break Aiden out. One was the trainee, and he was obviously the inside man. I told him that I saw him face down and how I had his dog tags. I told him I went for his gun and shot the intruder. I told him Aiden was still with us.

"I guess I owe you my life." He smiled.

"I guess so," I said, loving that smile and so happy he was alive.

He reached up and touched my face. "You know what they say about owing someone your life."

"Yep, you have to owe them yours."

"I'd give it to you if I could. But it isn't mine." He let his hand drop. "Try to forget about me Karen. Try to forget about us. It's the best way. You saw what happened tonight." Then he turned his head. "I don't know if I would have been able to handle it if he had killed you."

"But he didn't, Owen. I'm right here, and I'm going to stay. Can't you see that?"

"No, Karen. Fisher. Please, my head hurts."

I wanted him to embrace me, but I had to keep him talking. "What about Fatima? Will we get her back now?"

He took a deep breath and said, "On my desk."

I went to his desk, which was a mass of chaotic papers. I sorted through them until I stopped on two blown-up black and white photos. They were blurry and might have been taken with a smuggled camera, but it was Fatima.

I gasped. She sat on the floor completely stripped of clothing, and her hands were chained to a wall. By the angles of her fingers, I could tell they had been broken. I shuddered at the pain that must be causing her. There was a second picture taken from a front angle. She lay in a puddle that might be her own blood. Her nose was broken, and her face was a mess of swollen tissue. "Oh God," I muttered and caught the bile from escaping seconds before I threw up. "Oh, God. No. We have to get her back."

Owen's voice was a hoarse whisper, "If there's anything to get back."

"I want to work with George on Aidan," I said, pushing back any doubt I had about our mission. This was his life, and now it was mine too.

Owen sighed. "I'll assign you with him, but you have to stop any doubt about what we're doing. Can you do that?" He stared at me then.

"Yes," I whispered, and this time he looked away before I did.

ALL IN

For the next few days, I went to help George administer the IV with Zap to Aidan. I helped him hold up the picture of his brother Marcus while Aidan listened to recorded messages telling him Marcus was his enemy. Aidan squirmed against the arm shackles, and his whole body shook, but then George gave him a shot and he calmed down.

I brought Aidan food and unfastened his shackles so he could move about. He shot a hand out to scratch me, but George and Smith grabbed him back, and after a while he walked around without incident. Owen stayed in his office for the week.

By the end of the week, Aiden was gone, and I sat with George praying for Fatima's safe return. Smith was the one who came to tell us she had died in the hospital from the injuries she'd sustained.

Another recruit came to take her place, but I didn't talk to her. Like Owen had warned, don't get too close to anyone. He beefed up security as well. We had three new guards, and one was posted on the front door at all times. That pleased me because I didn't know if I could go through another attack.

I'd had dreams that Farid's ghost shot at me through the bars of my room. But at least Mr. Mackee had stopped haunting me with his deadpan eyes, whispering, "What the hell, Karen? What the hell?" No, the night I took Farid's life, I felt my students slipping away. I'd confronted my fears, and even though it might have made me a target for retaliation, my students finally rested in peace in my mind.

Two nights later, I heard jailers talking and someone crying on the main floor. At first I thought I must be dreaming until I sat on my cot for a moment and listened again.

Heavy boots, Owen and Smith's muted voices. The cry of a wounded animal or a child. I sprang from my cot but only saw the heel of a man's boot disappear from the low, yellow night light.

By the time I slid out of my cage, the group had disappeared, no doubt into Owen's office. The guard standing outside the door that exited the mess to the offices dissuaded me from storming the door.

Sighing, I retreated back to my room. I would find Owen the next morning and ask about what I'd heard. We hadn't talked since that night when he asked me to forget about him. To forget about us.

I rolled over to face the wall and try to sleep. But Owen filled my mind. He loved me. Loved whoever I was now. Maybe that love would give me the strength to be someone now. But now I wanted him with every cell of my body. I wanted him. He'd said you couldn't count on anyone, but I wanted to count on him to help breathe this new life into me.

I sensed something behind me. I jerked back. Owen stood at my door. Finally, he was coming to me. All that yearning flooded me for his arms, his touch, and his reassurance. I wanted to hear him tell me he loved me. For him to surrender to his feelings.

I bolted to the door, and then the three kids came into view. Two boys, maybe nine and seven, and a little girl of about five. What? Each child's wide dark eyes tracked me. Their brows furrowed like big question marks.

"Owen?" I said trying to repress the warm longing between my thighs.

"You need to move to an apartment we fixed on the top floor," Owen said.

"Who... ?" I couldn't finish.

"We need you to watch them."

"Why? Where did—"

He cut me off. "No time now." He turned away. "Just get your clothes. The kids are tired and scared. We need to move—get them settled."

"Where did they come from?" I asked, not moving.

He turned back. "Iraq. Now, it's late. Let's go."

I clutched a bag full of my clean clothes and my cell phone and followed Owen. His hand enveloped the tiny girl's, which disappeared completely in his huge one. My heart hurt for him and the daughter he'd probably never get to see again. He'd make a good father. The two boys followed behind them, and I trailed the four.

The door opened on the third floor to a large open space with a couch, loveseat, flat-screen television, dining room, and kitchen. A hallway trailed off to the side, which I imagined must lead to bedrooms.

A picture window facing the front of the prison caught my attention. I could see out to where we were, but all was darkness. As if sleepwalking, my feet moved over soft carpet, something I'd missed. I looked up at a moon and countless stars. I knew we were not in the city, and hadn't Smith said we were in Palmdale? Still in California but in the desert, nothing but tumbleweed around us.

"Help me put them to bed." Owen had lifted the sleepy girl onto his shoulder, and she had finally stopped sniffling. He veered off to the side hallway, and I tore my gaze from the land in front of the building. It's funny that only eight weeks before, I wanted to escape, but now, faced with the world outside, I didn't want it after all. Maybe I never had.

Four doors spilled into the narrow, carpeted hallway. Owen elbowed his way into the first door. The only light came from the soft glow of a nightlight. The bed was made up with a pink comforter, and to the side was a small white desk.

Owen went to the bed and slowly lowered the child to it. She opened her eyes and let out a whimper. Her hands, like a small, trapped bird, struggled to grasp him, not wanting to let go. "It's okay, sweetheart." His words tugged at my heart. Had he said them to his own child? Had she held on to him as he tried to leave her life? "You're just going to bed."

The boys moved toward the bed as if to see whether they needed to defend their sister. The oldest sat on the bed and touched his sister's leg. The little girl leaned toward him with her hands outstretched. "No. Your room is next door," Owen said patting the boy's shoulder.

The boy reached toward his sister, and Owen worked to separate them. "Karen, come here and hold the girl. I have the boys." With that, he lifted the oldest and scooped up the younger brother, who acted like he'd been cemented to the floor. He dragged them away. I saw the boys flail and the oldest try to bite Owen as I went to the shrieking girl.

Pushing her cheek to my chest, I rocked her as she wept. "It's okay. No one is going to hurt you. You're safe." She tried to reach her hands around me to get to her brothers. I heard scuffling behind me, but I didn't look around. The door closed. I pressed the girl's ear to me to block off the yelling and banging the boys made, which left her trembling and pushing away from me.

A door slammed down the hall, and more yelling and crying erupted from beyond our room. I held my own tears in check for the little children. They were younger than the kids who'd died at my school, but the screams felt the same. What the hell was Department G doing with these kids?

The little girl finally seemed to go limp in my arms, but when I attempted to ease her to the bed, she started and clutched me. Owen opened the door behind me, bringing on a new set of sobs from the girl. "I'll see you in the morning," he said.

I whirled around still clutching the terrified child. "Wait a minute. We need to talk. What do you want me to do?" He didn't answer. I gritted my teeth. "Who are they? What do I do with them?"

He held up a key. "They're locked in for the night. Get some sleep. Your room is the last door on the right."

"No way." I moved to get up and the girl cried harder. "You're not leaving me here alone with them. And locking the boys in. What if they need to use the restroom? Are you crazy?"

"Good night, Fisher." He turned to leave.

I started to stand up, but the girl gripped me and wailed. I sighed, and because I didn't want to raise my voice and alarm the child more, I whispered, "You bastard. You unbelievable bastard," as he closed the door.

When the girl finally fell asleep, I walked on legs that felt full of electricity to the hallway. No noise came from the room that the boys occupied, so I turned and headed for the door, for Owen.

The handle didn't turn. He had locked me in. New anger welled inside me. Then I remembered he had a key. I whirled around and stubbed my toe dashing around looking for a light switch. The light illuminated the kitchen counter, the gas range. No key. I yanked open wooden cabinets on either side of the oven. Owner's manuals for the appliances, dish towels with the price tags still hanging from them, and utensils. No keys.

Gritting my teeth, I stormed back to the girl's bedroom. I stepped on something hard and pointed. I reared back, gasping in pain. On the floor a metal object shimmered in a slice of moonlight. I snatched up a skeleton key.

I went back to the door and jammed it in the key-hole. It didn't turn. No way. My fist came down on the wooden panel before I stopped for fear of waking the kids. The thought of racking my manicured nails over Owen's cheek flitted through my mind. I'd paint my nails red with his cowardly blood.

Shaking, I turned to the living room. Exhaustion mingled with rage, and I slumped down into the easy chair facing the picture window. The ground was pitch.

What had Smith said? "I can't wait to get out of this damn Palmdale desert." I'd seen a sign for "102nd Street". I knew where I was. I could escape. A million stars dotted the black sky. If I had a rope, I could rappel down the side of the building, and if I had an M-16 I could bash the outside guard's head in. Then I could take his keys, enter the building, and bust into Owen's office. Once there, I'd threaten him until he came up to the apartment, where I'd lock him in for two days. I sighed. If I had some rope and some guts.

I must have dozed because when I pried my eyes opened, red and yellow streaks adorned the horizon, and the little girl stood in front of me clutching her blanket. Oh, damn. I had to stifle a cry, but the girl's lower lip quivered none-the-less.

I got up and knelt before her. "It's okay, sweetie. Why don't we find your brothers and get you all something to eat. Do you like cereal?" I'd seen a box of Cap'n Crunch in the cupboard when I'd been looking for the keys.

Her blank teary look me told me she didn't speak English. I picked her up. She stiffened and reared away from me. Her ribs protruded through her thin cotton shirt as she arched her back as though trying to get away and levitate. My grip loosened so I almost dropped her. "I'm not going to hurt you." She twisted making sounds like a wounded puppy. Tightening my grip, I hugged her despite her struggle.

She kneed me in the stomach as I bent to retrieve the key from the carpet where I must have dropped it. My courage faltered once I got to the door where the boys were. Was I unlocking the cage to a lions' den? There were three of them and only one of me.

I cursed Owen again for whatever insane plan he had that involved scaring innocent children.

As I opened the door, my nostrils were assaulted with the smell of urine. The bed mattress was overturned and the lamp and end table knocked to the floor. Drawers were opened and dumped. In the back corner, the boys were curled up together in a tight ball.

The girl buried her face in my neck as if the scene frightened her. I sighed and felt extremely tired. Lowering her to the floor, I entered the room and picked up the mattress and drawers.

Then nausea overcame me. I ran into the bathroom ricocheting from the doorframe to the sink before knocking my knees again the toilet and throwing up. Pressing a wet washcloth to my forehead, I pushed down the new dread I felt. I was in trouble, and I couldn't tell Owen. Not yet.

The boys entered the kitchen as I scrambled eggs, made toast, and gulped orange juice to settle my stomach. I had eyed the bacon, but the thought of that grease made me want to hurl again.

The older boy grunted something to his sister, and she came to his side. Grape jelly leaked from the corners of her mouth where she'd missed with her toast.

"Hey. Glad you're awake. How about some breakfast?" I tried for the cheeriest voice I could manage through my headache and upset stomach.

The younger of the boys came forward, and his brother whipped out a hand to hold him back. Gruff words were exchanged, and I realized he was speaking French. The jihadi François was from France. Were these his weak links?

"Okay, suit yourselves." I placed two equal portions of eggs on the plates with some toast and went to pour the orange juice in small red cups. By the time I turned back around, the little boy had scrambled onto a chair and attacked the food.

He smiled up at me with egg and toast on his face. He had a sparkle in his milk-chocolate-colored eyes. His brother stayed rooted with a grimace and a furrowed brow. Good morning, sunshine, I thought, and next: I'm going to kill Owen.

And speak of the devil, the key sounded in the lock, and we all spun around to stare at the door as it opened. Owen stood there accompanied by the French trainee.

I became speechless, and he motioned to the trainee. "This is Tomas. He can speak to the kids." It was then that Owen looked at me, and I saw in his eyes that I must look a mess. My hand immediately went to my hair, and I patted it down.

Tomas began speaking with the children. The older boy yelled and threw up his arms in a tantrum. His sister leaned against my leg and gripped it as if I could protect her.

"What are you doing with them?" I asked Owen.

"Tomas will take the older boy. We need you to entertain the little ones."

"Why?" I asked.

Owen sighed. "I have orders just like you, Fisher."

"Are you going to do to him what you did to Aidan?"

"Hopefully it won't come to that." "Hopefully." Was he really considering drugging a child?

Owen turned to Tomas. "Okay, take him out of here." The boy didn't go quietly. He pummeled the men with kicks and punches. The other two flew at them with arms and legs and mouths. "Karen, get a hold of them," Owen yelled between gritted teeth.

I almost wanted to laugh and do nothing to help. Let him get beaten up by three babies. But little girl's tears and snot tore at my heartstrings, and I bent to scoop her in my arms. "It's okay, baby girl." I hugged her close.

At the door, Tomas shoved little boy back and called him "Samuel.

"What is her name?" I asked as the door closed.

"Amira," Tomas answered through the wood.

Samuel and Amira. Samuel slumped against the door, pounding on it and crying, "François." That must be his brother's name. The older one was named after his dad.

Unable to bear their tears, I went to the television set and found some cartoons. Soon both kids had joined me on the couch. And sometime later, the three of us dozed off, both children curled up in balls under my arms.

I woke with a start to Sponge Bob yelling at Mr. Krabs. I looked at the clock. It was 11 a.m. When was Owen coming back? And what then?

Amira stared up at me. We couldn't lie around in our pajamas all day, and both kids smelled of urine and that breezy smell of unwashed kid . "How would you like to take a bath, and then maybe you can help me make some cookies?"

She held my hand as I filled the tub with water. Samuel stayed rooted to the couch. Maybe he wanted to be there as soon as François returned. When the bathtub was full, Amira shook her head to going in. I added bubbles and splashed them around, but it was still no deal. I would have loved to get in the water. I was dirty, and my bones ached. Finally, I bribed her into the water with some chocolate I found in the cabinet.

I leaned my arms into the warm water and splashed the little girl. Then I took handfuls of water and drenched myself, welcoming the closest I could come to a bath at that moment. We put bubbles in each other's hair and giggled. The warm water eased the tension in my limbs. I was about to pull her out and wrap her in a towel before drying my soaked clothes and body when Samuel appeared, pushing the door open. I wrapped a towel around myself and asked, "You want to get in too?" I held out the remaining piece of candy bar and pointed to the tub. He slipped out of his shirt and pants and joined his sister. I watched as bubbles and chocolate shoved in his mouth. They laughed and splashed each other. I wanted to go get dressed but remembered that sometimes kids drown in water. However, they did have each other. What would a real mother do? I slipped out, grabbed my clothes and changed before returning to rub shampoo in Samuel's long black hair.

François didn't return until after dinner, and that coward Owen didn't bring him. The boy's eyes were red, and he was shaking. He let me lead him to a chair at the dining room table, where I poured him some orange juice.

Amira came over and leaned her head in his lap. He didn't seem to notice her as his hands clutching the glass stirred the juice like a blender. Juice slopped over the lip of the glass and splashed on Amira. As he drank, the glass clinked against his teeth.

I finally got all three kids to sleep by placing their blankets on the floor next to each other. I slept over them in the easy chair and worried that I'd never be able to handle this mothering routine. François woke us all up about midnight when he began to moan and yell in his sleep. Amira immediately jumped in my lap, but Samuel shook his brother. François swung out at Samuel, and Samuel let out a yell.

I grabbed the little boy up as François opened his eyes and took in what he'd done. I got some ice for the welt on Samuel's cheek. It was an hour before I got everyone separated in their own private chair tents so they would sleep apart.

When Tomas came for François the next day, the younger children didn't protest alone. I stood in front of a nearly comatose François and said, "No. He's not going."

"But I 'ave my orders," Tomas said.

"I don't care what you have. He's not going."

"You will 'ave to get Mr. Kafferdy up 'ere then."

"I guess you will."

With that, Mr. Tomas went to get Mr. Kafferdy. Owen appeared five minutes later. "Fisher, come on. We haven't touched a hair on his head."

"It's what you've done inside his head that I'm concerned with. Do you see that welt on Samuel's face? François did that accidentally."

"Okay, so we keep him isolated from them."

I took a deep breath. "Oh, that's so much better. No. There has to be a different way."

Owen's shoulders slouched. "Okay, come. You and the other kids can come with him."

"Their names are Amira, Samuel, and François."

"Don't get too close, Karen. I warned you about that."

"Well at least you remember my name." I felt smug with my sarcasm.

I didn't miss the roll of Owen's eyes. We exited, but still François held back. Samuel and Amira clutched my hand, but Samuel kept looking back to François as if his brother might disintegrate into dust if he didn't keep an eye on him. How easily little ones forgave anything, even an unprovoked smack to the face.

On the ground floor we went into the office across from Owen's. It was a mini theater with projector, bucket seats, and a movie screen. The children clambered over the seat as if excited by the prospect of watching more cartoons.

I feared that Sponge Bob wouldn't be making a return appearance. In fact, when the lights dimmed and the projector flickered, pictures flashed as if in a subliminal suggestion experiment. I caught glimpses of jihadists beheading people, of children screaming and people being shot. Most of the words were in French, but the screaming was universal. Amira buried her little head into my side. Samuel's gaze flicked between the screen and François. But François stared blankly ahead. Amira soon began to cry, and I stood up so my silhouette made a shadow puppet across the screen. "Enough. Stop. You're upsetting them."

The lights flooded the room, but still the images flicked across my white T-shirt and blinded me. "Take out the younger kids then, but the boy stays with Tomas," Owen said.

I wanted to protest, but I needed the little ones to get out before they had nightmares that kept us all up for days. I had to yank Samuel's hand before he'd leave François.

We all waited, biting our lips for the return of François. I made a meal of meatloaf, potatoes, and carrots with sliced apples for dinner once François returned, but mostly we picked at it. I wondered if the little ones had the same thoughts I did. What has he seen? What will he do now?

When I finally got everyone down on their pillows by leaving the television on, I made a decision. I packed a backpack with a change of clothes, a flashlight, three bottles of water, and granola bars. Then I lay down to close my bloodshot eyes and quiet my sick stomach.

THE ESCAPE

The metal door sounded hollow under my knuckles as I rapped on Owen's door. The girl's tiny hand cooled my palm. I swallowed the fear welling up in me. He opened the door and rubbed his eyes as if waking from a dream.

"Karen? What's up?"

"I'm walking out of here, and I'm taking them with me." I pointed to the boys huddling together behind me. When I looked back and met Owen's eyes, a longing warmed me. His hair had grown out slightly, and stubble lined his angular chin. I wanted to stay with him, to have him love me again. To walk through the rest of my life with him.

"You can't. We need them. Their father has killed dozens of innocent people. Think of your students. They're our bargaining chips. I can't let you. I won't."

I swallowed the ball of angry at the mention of my students. "They're more than a bargaining chip. You intend to use them to kill their father. You can't do it. I won't let you."

"I can't let them go. I can't let you go."

"Then you're going to have to use that pistol you carry, because I'm leaving." I blinked back tears that threatened to give away my feelings. My resolve was as thin as a tissue, one breath away from ripping to shreds. That's the way it is with cowards, but I gritted my teeth. I couldn't save my own kids, but I could save these three.

He sighed. "I thought you understood. I hoped I could make you understand. It's the only way to stop this terrorism."

"No." My voice shook. "Violence begets violence. Gandhi said, 'Be the change you want to see in the world.' I want to be peace."

"Gandhi—what does he know? He never had to face the dirtbags we do now. He never held his brothers in his arms as they gasped for one last breath to send love to a family they left behind. And why? All because some terrorist shot an RPG at men who only wanted to make the world a better place. Gandhi's dead, Karen. I say if you aren't part of the solution, you're part of the problem."

"Never-the-less, I have to follow my conscience."

"Fisher—Karen—please." He reached for me. His fingertips tickled the fine hairs of my arm. "Maybe I shouldn't have stuck you with them. There are other jobs. I'll find you something else."

"No. This isn't right, Owen. We're walking out that door. You can shoot me in the back if you want to, but we're going."

His hands shook. "What are you going to do out there? How do you intend to get them home? Take them to the police?"

He was right.

"I'll give you twenty-four hours to clear out," I said. "Then I'm going to get these kids back to their parents."

"If you feel that strongly, I'll have someone come pick them up. You don't have to do this. We'll find another way."

My lips buckled. "No, Owen. I can't stay. I'm—" What would he say? Would he beg me to stay? Would I have the strength to go anyway? "I'm pregnant."

He released my arm. "Wait. What?" He searched my face as if looking for the punchline. "How?" Then the memory of the hotel room in Spain where he hadn't worried about a condom must have returned to him because he asked, "Is... is it... is it mine?"

"Would that make any difference?"

As he looked at me, his eyes flooded with tears. Before he shook his head, he looked down.

"I didn't think so." I wanted to hug him—to wish him well and tell him we'd be okay. If I was honest, I wanted to change his mind or have him throw me over his shoulder and force me to stay. But there were the kids. He took my phone and two wadded-up bills from his jeans pocket and handed them to me. He was letting me go. I momentarily thought of his ex-wife, Brenda, and the money she refused to take to ease his conscience.

He inched away and pivoted before departing into the office and slowly closed the door. The man I loved was turning his back on me for the last time. I wanted him to turn around. I wanted him to say he'd go with us. We could be a family. Me, him, and our unborn child. But behind the door, I thought I heard or imagined I heard him whisper, "I love you." Then the deadbolt clicked into place, and he was gone. I looked down at the money, two hundred-dollar bills. That was my payoff. That was what I was worth to him.

I forced back the tears flooding my eyes. Biting my lip, I turned with the three kids and ambled to the door. It was then that I realized bravery doesn't only come at the end of a gun or with a bomb strapped to you. No, sometimes bravery is doing what you know is right even when it scares the hell out of you.

Outside the front door the security guard stopped us. "Where do you think you're going?" It was George. "Karen, what are you—" He looked from me to the kids. He lowered the gun. "What... what are you doing?"

I sniffed in the dry, still air. "I'm taking these kids and leaving."

"No, you can't. I've been ordered to shoot anyone who tries to leave or enter without permission."

"Then you're going to have to shoot me, George, because I'm leaving." And suddenly his gun didn't scare me half as much as leaving Owen did. "We're leaving. Owen knows. He's letting me go."

"Why?"

"I can't just sit back and let Department G kidnap and torture kids."

He sighed. "But they'll only grow up to be terrorists like their fathers. Didn't you see what they did to Fatima?" His hand shook slightly. "We have to stop it. Better drugs than bombs. They won't stop killing even our own kids. And if you leave, the police will want to know where you got those kids."

"I know that."

"You can get us all arrested."

"Then you'd better pack and leave."

"You can't mean that. This is what we've been training for. I've... we've got to make her life count for something."

"All life counts for something, George." I smiled through the tears. "I killed a man to save a life. I know what that means, but they"—I pointed at the upturned faces of the three kids to stay strong—"didn't do anything, and torturing them is something they do when they enter a school and shoot all the innocent kids."

"I can't let you go. I won't." He lifted the gun.

"Then, my friend, you are going to have to shoot me in the back. I'll never forget you, but there is no chance in hell you're stopping us." I turned to walk away.

I heard his heavy footfall behind me, and then he was in front of me blocking my path.

His gun was slung over his shoulder. He opened his arms, and I embraced him. His camouflage jacket smelled like campfire, and his arms felt strong and sure around me. He pulled away and sniffed. "Take care of yourself. I wish you luck out there."

"You too, George, and I hope you always follow your conscience, whatever decisions you make." We strode away without getting shot. We had a long walk ahead of us. "We're going home." I told the kids as if to convince myself. "We're going home." To them, that was probably a familiar place, but not so for me.

The flashlight illuminated the path twenty feet ahead of us. Our shoes kicked up the dry, packed dirt of the unpaved road. How far was it exactly? A coyote bayed at the moon, and the boys bumped up against me. The slight breeze made me shiver, or was it the fact that I was leaving—leaving Owen and the certainty that Department G offered me? But where was I going? I fingered the cell phone in my pocket. Steven. I needed to call Steven. He'd come get me. I was counting on it.

Amira tugged at my sweatpants and held up her arms for me to carry her. The last thing I wanted was the burden of more weight, but we were moving slowly, and I wanted to get to that abandoned motel I'd seen before the sun came up. We were moving targets.

Could Farid's friends have scouted the place out or called a hit out for me? And even if they hadn't, I'd never be able to explain to a cop or a random driver why I was out in the desert roaming like Moses with three small children. So I reached exhausted arms down and picked up the girl.

Samuel was next to tug on my pants. He yawned and put up his hands. I couldn't carry both of them. I wanted to curse Owen for not offering to drive us. I knew letting us leave was the most he could handle, but what a coward to let us brave this alone.

I sat down cross-legged and pulled from my backpack the bottles of water. The children sat around me, and we took turns taking drinks. The day was turning gray at the edges. How much farther did we have to walk? I glanced back at the three-story cell block. It had to be at least a mile from us by then.

The time on my phone told me we'd been walking forty minutes. We had maybe half a mile left. I could keep walking for the next twenty minutes, but could they? Samuel lay a small shaggy head down on my knee and seemed to fall asleep immediately.

"We have to keep going," I said. "We only have about twenty minutes left."

François nodded as though he understood. Maybe it was being outside or away from Department G that woke him out of his comatose state, but his eyes seemed clearer. Amira nestled next to me as if she wanted to sleep like her brother.

After downing two granola bars so I wouldn't puke, I got up and pushed my three responsibilities ahead. One hour later we scratched our ankles on the tumble weed and thorns in the brown dust in front of the Ran- ch Motel. I herded the kids toward the back of the building, feeling every foxtail that had attached itself to my socks and sweatpants.

I drew a fingertip over the plastic of the phone. Did I have any right to call him? Did I have any choice? And I knew he'd come, but what would I say? Get some guts and just do it. I called Steven and, holding my breath, waited.

One ring. Another. Is it too early? I looked at the phone's face. 0630. Maybe, but I couldn't stay out in the open long. I was about to hang up when he answered. "Hello?"—a question.

"Steven—" I let it hang.

"Karen, is that... I've been trying to call you. Where are... are you okay?"

His answer was a jumble of questions, and I let out my held breath. "Yes. It's me. I'm sorry, Steven. I'm okay, but I need your help."

"Where are you?"

"I'm in the Palmdale desert."

"In California?" He must still have been half asleep to ask that. He caught his mistake because he added, "I just thought you were in rehab in Mexico."

"I need you to come pick us up."

"Us?"

Shoot, I must have been exhausted to let that slip. I meant to wait to ex- plain the kids. He might want to know too much. And God help me, I didn't want to explain Owen or Department G. A part of me wanted Owen and George to get away before I had to go to the police to explain what happened to me. A part of me would feel safer knowing Department G was out there. Knowing he was out there.

I glanced at the three yawning children who looked like they had wandered the desert for days. "I have some kids with me."

"Kids? What's going on, Karen?"

"I'll tell you everything once you get here. Please, Steven."

"Do you know what day it is?"

"No," I admitted and felt stupid I hadn't thought to look at the date on my phone. But in my defense, I had been a little busy.

"It's Christmas Eve."

"Christmas Eve?" I'd left at the end of October. So I'd been gone two months.

"I'm supposed to go to dinner with my parents at two. And they're setting me up with a date."

I felt like a fist squeezed my heart. Steven's parents had never really liked me. Of course he'd move on. But after only two months? Well, hadn't I moved on to Owen? It just never occurred to me that Steven might not be there when I got back.

"I'm so sorry, Steven. I wouldn't ask you if there was any other way. If I had anyone else." And suddenly I realized just how alone I was.

"Okay. I'll come. Where are you exactly?" My eyes watered as I thanked God I could still count on Steven.

"At an abandoned hotel called Ranch Motel. It's on 102nd Ave in the Palmdale desert."

"How did you get there?"

"Please just come. I'll explain everything."

Christmas Eve, I thought when I hung up. I'd be spending my Christmas in the police station. Would they arrest me for kidnapping? Would they believe me? And my mother—would she forgive me, tomorrow being Christmas and all?

Steven's Ford pickup rolled over the gravel, spitting it into the air. I emerged from the rear of the decaying hotel with the three kids huddling around me. Steven's eyes said it all as he drank in my tired face and took in the muscle tone in my arms. I hustled the kids in between us, and he took off, only giving me confused stares.

We drove in silence until we reached the highway. Then Steven, who clutched the steering wheel so tight I feared his knuckles would turn permanently white, said, "So you going to tell me what you're doing out in the goddamn desert?"

I sighed. "I wrapped the car around a pole the night of the interview. When I woke, I was in a former prison cell but not arrested. I was as confused as you are. I was told that I'd been recruited by an organization called Department G."

"Wait. You wrapped your car around a pole and woke up in a prison cell. Do you realize how crazy you're sounding? If I detected any alcohol on your breath, I might be able to understand this."

"Do you think I understood it? You think I believed it at first?"

"You look tired but tanned, and you look like you lost weight. Why did you say you were in Mexico in rehab?"

"I didn't tell you that." Amira tugged on my arm. I looked down at her, and she pointed to François. Tears leaked from his eyes. "It's okay." I patted her leg and tapped François on the shoulder. The boy didn't move. "You're safe now. No one is going to hurt you. I'm taking you home."

"Where are these kids from?" Steven took his foot off the accelerator, slowing the car down.

"Department G took them from their home to exert pressure on their jihadi father. As I was trying to tell you, Department G works below the law to fight terrorism."

"Wait, what?"

"I know. You already said it sounds crazy. And I can't help how crazy the truth sounds. You know me, Steven. When have I ever lied to you?"

"Well, the last few times we spoke, you said you weren't drunk. Hadn't had a drink. It wasn't a problem."

"But… " What could I say to make him believe? "Look, we already established I got drunk. I went through something, but I'm sober now, and I'm telling you the truth." My voice was a plea.

François began to moan and rock as Steven's voice rose. "What is wrong with that kid?"

"Department G wanted to use him to kill his father."

"Oh my God, this just gets better. Department G kidnaps you and these kids to kill terrorists. What are you all, the new Seal Team Six?"

I couldn't answer as I thought of the old Seal Team Six, and one member in particular. Steven went on, "Who did they want you to kill? Jihadi John, or that guy who attacked your school? No, he's already dead. Do they know you didn't kill him?"

We traveled through a city of box-like buildings called Lancaster. Traffic had gotten heavy probably with people getting their last-minute holiday needs before stores closed for Christmas.

I thought about what Steven said and about Farid, the man I did kill. "No one. They didn't ask me to kill anyone. But I have killed a man." I bit my lip at the last word.

Steven pulled to the side of the highway. He threw open his door and stepped out. Little puffs of dirt pooled around his Vans sneakers as he paced. His mouth became a tight line, and his shoulders bunched around his neck. Then he put his hands to his head and shook. I killed a man. It was in self-defense—or was it? Was I so far gone that those distinctions didn't matter? The truth was, two months ago that was something I could never have conceived of.

Amira let out a whimper, bringing me back into the car. I plastered a smile on my face and ignored the trembling in my hand. "What do you guys say we stop at a restaurant and get lunch and hot fudge sundaes?" I glanced at my watch; it was 11:30.

I'd seen one cop car and was nervous that Steven's pacing and obvious agitation might alert another. But I gnawed my lip and tried to speak calmly. "We can stop at a Baskin Robbins. Have you ever been to a Baskin Robbins? It's so much fun." Amira and Samuel looked at me with a smile but quickly gave a cautious glance out the window toward Steven. "Oh him, he's just a big butt head. Don't worry about him. He really likes kids." I rubbed my stomach and hoped what I was saying was true.

Then I opened the door and slipped onto the litter-strewn shoulder to talk to Steven. He stopped pacing and stood in front of me. "What? What do you want me to say?"

"Nothing. But please get back into the car before a cop stops."

"Maybe one should stop. We could sort this all out right here and now, Karen." He put his hands on his hips and gave me a twisted grimace.

"Maybe so. I don't know. But what I do know is a week ago I was in a place I thought I could stay, working for a cause I thought I could be a part of."

"Murdering people?"

"No, Steven, preventing other students like mine from being slaughtered. Because"—my lips buckled—"I couldn't save them. They all died, and I couldn't save them. You were right when you said I died that day too." I swallowed the lump in my throat so I could go on. "Maybe you could have been stronger and come back from that. I couldn't. But I've changed. A man pointed a gun at one of my friends, and I killed him. Shot him. I can't change the past. But I'm asking you to forgive me—help me—even though I haven't completely forgiven myself." Tears brimmed in my eyes.

His expression began to soften, and he pulled me into an embrace. I felt his warm chin against my head. My tears soaked his T-shirt. "Okay," he said. "Let's go eat and then maybe stop somewhere, and I'll listen to everything." He pulled back to look into my eyes. "Okay?"

I sighed, and we got back in the car. After lunch, to my surprise, we stopped at a hotel and checked in. It was tricky with three kids, but we got two adjacent rooms, and I put the television on for the kids. Steven and I opened the door between the rooms and sat on the two twin beds, our knees slightly touching.

Now that he would listen, I was nervous about how much to tell him, so I started from the beginning. I told him about George, Fatima, and Daisy, who took out Muhammed John.

"I read about that in the LA Times. Lerdo Prison, a riot, and a fundamental Muslim leader getting killed," he said.

"That was Department G."

"This Department G is still hard for me to wrap my head around. Kind of like the X-Files."

"It took me weeks to understand it." Then I told him about our missions to Spain and Virginia. I skirted around Owen, only mentioning he was the leader and had been the sole survivor of Seal Team Six.

"You were going to stay," Steven said, not a question.

"I stopped having the nightmares about the kids dying. I didn't need a drink to get through the day."

"I couldn't do that for you?" he asked.

"I couldn't do that for myself."

"Did you love him?" The question threw me for a moment, and that hesitation told Steven everything. I clutched my stomach and had a hard time finding the words to answer.

Finally, I just nodded. Steven shot up. "Oh God, Karen. Did you sleep with him?"

Another nod. Steven slapped his forehead. "Shit, shit. What the hell? Why did you even call me? Fuck. I should just leave now." He grabbed his keys and headed for the door. He paused and, peered back before he went out slamming the door behind him.

Biting my lip, I crossed over into the kids' room. The cartoon Rudolph the Red-Nosed Reindeer was on the television, and I wondered if I should be out shopping for their presents. Stupid; Steven had left me, I'd left Owen, and I didn't know what the hell I'd do next. The one thing I couldn't do was disappoint the kids with no Santa Claus. No, Virginia, there's no Santa Claus. Maybe I really was insane.

Steven had said he had a dinner with his parents at two p.m. And they'd set him up with a date. Of course that was where he was going. "Okay, kids. Let's go. We're going Christmas shopping."

We had no car, so we walked to the Walgreens across the street. I bought wrapping paper with elves on it and some with angels. Amira liked the dolls, so I got her one and, while she was preoccupied, slipped another in the cart, to wrap from Santa. Samuel was fascinated by the candy in the stockings, so I bought three of them. François stopped at the plastic guns, but I decided, given his recent experiences, that I'd steer clear of any toys of destruction and got two matchbox cars for the boys . Then I poured more candy in the cart.

Great, I was about to embark on motherhood, and I was already rotting the teeth of three trusting kids. I almost asked if there was a bathroom where I could sit and be alone to cry my eyes out. Instead, thoughts of abandoning the kids and returning to Owen flitted through my mind. On my left, the rows of liquor bottles shone from behind their glass cabinets. I licked my lips. I could buy a few just to take the edge off.

Amira tugged at my hand, and I looked down at her small round face as she held her Santa's helper Barbie up to me. I couldn't do that to the kids. It was time to stop leaning on liquor. I would stop thinking altogether and just act for their sake, and then there was my baby to consider. God, I was in so much trouble.

Stiffening my upper lip, I grabbed a white plastic tree and a box of ornaments and paid for the items. The sales-clerk said a cheery, "Have a Merry Christmas" as the door jingled and we exited.

If we hadn't paid for the rooms with Steven's credit card, I would have left the kids in the room and gone back to the Ran-ch Motel. But was he still there? I'd given Owen twenty-four hours. He was lost to me now, too. And the room would be traced back to Steven and I'd piled enough crap on him.

The kids played with Life Savers candy rolls and the doll while I wrapped the other gifts and hid them under my bed. They helped me decorate the tree, and we watched Miracle on 34th Street before Amira kissed my cheek and they all slipped into bed. I stayed awake in my room with the television muted.

Outside the window, Walgreens had closed. I licked my upper lip and put the curtain back in place. Too late to change my mind and go buy some wine. Thoughts of what came next raced through my mind like IEDs, buried and ready to explode. Okay, I thought clenching my shaking hands, I'll go to the police station and return the kids tomorrow. Then I'll turn myself in for killing Farid. I might spend the rest of my life in prison. No. Mom would certainly help me get a good attorney. I've seen enough "Law and Order" to know that without a body, murder was hard to prove. Wait—what about my student loans? How will I pay them back as a felon? How much did cons make while incarcerated? Oh, shut up.

ANOTHER CHANCE

I must have drifted asleep, because my eyes shot open and my heart raced as something cold touched my calf. I felt toes. A foot. I rolled around expecting Amira, but Steven wrapped his arms around me. His warm breath smelled slightly of eggnog. He stared into my eyes. "I think I loved you before I even met you. But do you love me? "

Unable to speak, I nodded.

He let me go and I turned to face him. "Remember in Afghanistan when I walked into the clinic?" he asked. I nodded again. "You were surrounded by all those men who were blown to bits by IEDs and shot and you were walking around helping everyone—even me. I had a cut that needed stitches, and your smile put me at ease." I bit my lip as he continued. "I think that's when I first fell in love with you." He propped himself up on his elbow. "We've been through some stuff. You always think you have to do it alone." He brushed a piece of hair from my forehead. "Even that shooting at the school. You couldn't let me in. Being with someone means you don't have to do any of it alone. Not anymore. Not if you don't want to." I hugged him close, still unable to answer.

Steven made love to me in that sweet, tender way of his. After, he asked, "Is it over, Karen? Are you back?"

At that moment, I thought of telling him about the baby but lost the courage. "I left Department G, if that's what you mean. I'm ready to go back home." I wasn't alone if I had Steven. I didn't want a life without a family— a life of never getting close to anyone. I'd deal with the baby issue later and hope Steven would be there when I did. "I'm sorry." I met his eyes.

"You were right," he said.

"About what?"

"I don't understand what it was like to nearly die in that school. I wish I did, but I don't. Just be straight with me: Are you back?"

I propped myself up on an elbow. "I want to be, Steven. There are things I've seen. Things I've done. But I'm ready for things to be what they are now. In a way, Department G saved me."

"Then tomorrow we go to the cops, and we never look back."

His gaze bore into me as if trying to read the response in my face. "Okay." Then I asked, "What did your parents say? What about that girl, the one they wanted to set you up with?"

"I went to dinner, but I didn't tell them where I was going afterward. She never tried to save lives in a war zone. She never had to fight terror and come out on the other side. She didn't act like my photos were the best thing she'd ever seen. And I don't think she needs me the way you do." He sat and extended his hand. "Hi, my name is Steven and I want to get to know you again."

I smiled and lay back down in his arms.

The next day the kids were shaking with excitement after I showed them how to rip the wrapping paper off their presents, and I regretted not getting one for Steven. There was a little ring box under the tree, and I swallowed the lump in my throat as Steven handed it to me.

"I didn't get you anything," I admitted as I tore the paper from the box. The diamond was small, but it shimmered as I held it up to the light.

Steven got down on one knee. "Karen Fisher, will you marry me?"

My lips buckled. "Please stand up." He frowned at my expression. I pressed the ring back into his hand. "Don't ask me now. Please wait until January 25th. Then give it back to me if you still want."

In his eyes I saw the hurt. "I want to ask you now. What is it? Is it him?"

"No." Although partly it was. It was the baby, and it was the father. "Please. I want you to be sure."

Thank God he didn't press. After a big breakfast at Denny's, we drove the rest of the way to the North Hollywood police station.

It was almost deserted, with three officers and one bleary-eyed prostitute. I gnawed on my lip as Steven led the kids and me to a desk toward the back.

"What can I do for you?" the twenty-something cop asked.

Steven pointed to me. It was now or never. "I want to get these kids back to their parents."

That began the hours of grueling questions. A female cop came and took the kids into another room, and Steven and I went into an interrogation room. I sat on the rock-hard chair in front of the scowling officer with the name tag that read "Van Trap." He clutched a ballpoint pen in his pale hand and said, "So start from the beginning."

He didn't interrupt me until I got to the part where I talked about Owen explaining the mission of Department G and hesitated. How much could I tell the cops? If I told this cop about going to Spain and helping in the kidnapping of Aidan, I'd be admitting to a felony and accusing Owen of one.

Officer Van Trap snapped his notebook shut and looked from me to Steven. His lips twisted back and forth like they didn't know what position to stay in. I thought I'd have a panic attack before he said, "So, you're saying this"—he made a show of consulting his notebook—"Department G kidnapped you. Like you say they kidnapped the three kids. You say this—" he put the notebook close to his nose and read—"Owen Kafferdy told you Department G is involved in terrorist hunting, and yet he kidnaps you and three kids." It wasn't a question, but I worried all the same about how to answer it. Could I keep out my part in Spain or my killing of Farid?

"Well," I stammered, "you may have read about my school, Monroe High School, being shot up and that I... well, I got out. Mr. Kafferdy thought I would be interested in stopping the terrorist who attacked my school. He kidnapped the kids to trap their father. He's a French jihadist. Their father, not Owen."

Now, Officer Van Trap didn't look at me as he read from his notebook. "Now you say Owen Kafferdy is the only surviving member of Seal Team Six." Officer Van Trap pinched his lips and added, "If you'll please go to the waiting room, I need to check on a few things."

Steven stood first and took my hand as we walked to a row of black vinyl seats across from a row of vending machines. "Merry Christmas," Steven said. "How about some turkey and gravy from one of these machines?"

I smiled for the first time all day. We ate candy bars and drank Dr. Peppers until Officer Van Trap motioned for us to reconvene in the interrogation room. I fixed my eyes on the sheets of copy paper clutched in his hand.

When we were seated again, he asked, "You claim it was Owen Kafferdy who was the leader of this terrorist fighting group? And you mentioned a Daisy Ross who killed civilians in Iraq? Then there was George Harrison, right?" I nodded. He set down a picture of a dark-haired naval officer. "Is this the infamous Kafferdy who did not die with the rest of his team in the helicopter crash that killed all the other members in 2012?" I attempted to ignore his sarcastic tone.

I leaned forward and picked up the picture of the unknown man. Then I quickly dropped it and moved away. "No." I shook my head. "No. That's not him." I looked to Steven. "It's not."

Steven took up the picture. "Are you sure?"

My lungs felt deflated, choking off my air supply so I could only nod.

"That's right," Officer Van Trap said. "Because Kafferdy died, and his family buried him in Arlington." Then he flipped over a second photo. "And Daisy Ross is in Fort Leavenworth." The African American woman in the photo was definitely not the Daisy Ross I met.

"This is wrong." I pushed back from his desk. "This is wrong. Go to Palm Desert and see it. You'll find the prison." I stood up.

"Please, Miss Fisher, sit," Officer Van Trap said.

But my whole body shook, and I had to pace. Overhead, the clock ticked so loudly, I thought I'd go crazy. I held my head in my hands and felt like I'd throw up any minute. Owen had lied to me. Oh God, I was pregnant with the child of a man I didn't even know. Who was Department G?

"Please sit, Miss Fisher. You're not going to faint on me or anything."

Steven stood and put his arm over my shoulder. He gently turned me around toward my vacated seat and applied pressure to my shoulder so I would sit.

Officer Van Trap hadn't finished. He produced a Beatles album cover. "But I did find George Harrison and Ringo, John, and Paul. Now let's try the truth."

"Michael?" I thought about the name his ex-wife had used. She'd definitely called him Michael. "Was Michael the name of one of the Seal Team Six members?"

"Lady, quit wasting my time and tell me who the kids are and how you got them, or I'll throw you in jail for kidnapping and filing a false police report."

Steven grabbed my hands as they shook. "Officer, we're going to stop right there, and I'm calling an attorney before she says another word."

Steven called his uncle, and he got me out of the police department with a promise not to darken their doorsteps again and a promise from Van Trap to get the kids home. When I said goodbye, Amira wet my shirt with her tears. Samuel crossed his arms and pouted. Only François seemed to go without a fight. But his tight lips and pale face told me he was scared, too.

Back home, Steven told no one I'd returned. At first, I loved the calm nothingness of my days, but eventually boredom set in. I wondered about Owen, George, Amira, Samuel, and François. Everyone was doing something, and I began to feel restless and useless. I'd left Department G because I wanted to be a champion for peace, but I needed to get out of my home to work toward that goal.

Then I got an idea. I searched the job vacancies at Amnesty International in Dakar, Senegal. There was a regional director's position. I'd decided I needed to be part of the solution, as Owen had said, but not in the way he meant. I approached Steven with my plan.

"Ghana? In Africa? Is that why you don't want to marry me right away?"

"No. It's just something I want to do."

"What about the baby?" he asked.

"How did you know... ?"

He shook his head. "You don't think I noticed you getting sick all the time?"

"After the baby. And we need to discuss that."

"No, we don't. We'll have the baby, and then we'll go to Africa to help people. If that's what you want. The newspaper would love to have a foreign correspondent, so I'll have plenty of work."

"But Steven, don't you think we should talk about this?"

"No, we'll get married and have our child and then go. That's all we need to talk about."

In the light of the kidnapping of Nigerian school girls and ISIS trying to get a stronghold in Nigeria, we'd be helping Amnesty International address women's rights. So six months after our son was born, we headed for the LAX airport.

Tom Bradley International Terminal was swarming with people. While waiting in the ticket line, I felt like someone was staring down at me. I looked up at the second floor and saw the form of a man, who had been leaning over the rail. I could just barely identify the scar on his cheek. Then he disappeared. I tried to follow him with my gaze, but he was swallowed up by a soccer team from Australia.

Steven had the baby sling over his shoulder and was jiggling Frankie up and down between handing me his passport and fishing out the baby's birth certificate from our luggage. As the April sun reflected off the silver railing, I realized the man must have been Owen or Michael or whatever his name was.

A sense of calm sadness washed over me. He'd never see his chocolate-eyed boy, but he was watching over him all the same. Department G had not been discovered in the Palmdale desert at Christmastime the year before, so they were still out there operating, or so I imagined.

As for us, we were giving back—me for killing a man. I'd use my teaching skills on kids who lived in huts and ran around without shoes. Students who hopefully wouldn't see the end of a gun. Steven would build a water sanitation unit.

FINAL RESOLUTION

Frankie played next to the wood that he and Steven had collected from the field. "That's the best wood we could find." Steven held up a scrawny limb. "Can we get a fire going with this?" He touched a crumpled dead leaf hanging on the branch to the end to Frankie's nose.

Our two-and-a-half-year-old son giggled. "Yes, Daddy. Big fire."

At that moment, the heavy African woman who acted as my assistant came into view. "Miss Karen, Miss Karen. For you." She held up a brown paper package tied with string and adorned with colorful foreign stamps. It had my name. I took it up and flipped it over.

Steven looked at me, and Frankie tried to grab the stick from his hand. "Daddy. Fire, Daddy. Make fire."

"Who's it from?" Steven asked.

"There's no return address." I picked at the string and, using my teeth, got a corner undone.

The rest of the string loosened, and I slipped it off. There was a note and a newspaper clipping. Steven eyed me, waiting for an explanation.

I marveled that Steven never asked about his son. The dimple on his chin or the blond hair that neither of us had, his dark eyes when we both had light ones, or even his stubborn, independent nature that contrasted with Steven's calm, patient manner. Despite it all, no father ever loved his child more, and when I'd mentioned a DNA test, he'd refused. He'd never wanted it confirmed.

I unfolded the note. It was on lined notebook paper, and I looked for the signature at the bottom first. It was from George.

"Who's it from?" Steven asked again.

"It's… " I thought about lying but Steven deserved the truth, and I'd made a promise I'd always be honest with him. I took a deep breath. "It's from George. Department G. Do you want to read it?" I held it out.

"No." He shook his head and turned to Frankie. "You want to go with Juma and catch a chicken?"

Frankie jumped up and down. "Yep. I get big one."

Steven took Frankie's hand and, after giving me one backward glance, walked away.

The letter was short. "Kafferdy asked me to send this to you if he ever failed to return from a mission." The newspaper clipping was an obituary from 2011. There was a photo of Michael Lafferdy in dress blues reported as killed in a helicopter crash that took over twenty members of his team. A shiver went down my spine. He had been a true ghost in my past. I traced his silhouette with my finger. I always thought I'd see him again one day.

I was about to throw the manila envelope in the fire when I realized it was too heavy to be empty. I peered into the depth of it to find something in a wad of tissue paper. I slid it into my palm. A rubber band held it together. I unwrapped it, and the dog tags fell into my hands. A note folded around them. "Fisher"—the word made my eyes water, and I read on through tears. "Give these to my son, if you want, or bury them wherever. I'm gone, and I'd like you to tell him about me someday."

I bit my lip and looked up. From the small pen behind our hut, Steven gazed in my direction and then looked back at our son, who ran after fluttering birds.

I forced a smile. Frankie grabbed Steven's arm. "Daddy. I almost got it. I almost." Then peals of laughter escaped from him. My son's shaggy blond hair fell over his wrinkled forehead as it often did when he was intent on getting his way. Steven picked him up and threw him over his shoulder, causing more giggles.

I buried the dog tags in my palm, then slipped them into my pocket. How do you tell your son he has two fathers? How do you break a decent man's heart to honor another's memory? No. Owen or Michael, whoever he was, would be a memory buried in my heart. He'd saved me once, but we had a son who needed to be saved too. Frankie deserved Steven, and that's where I'd leave it.

I walked to the fire pit and threw in the newspaper clipping, envelope, and note from George. Under the jacaranda tree, I dug a little hole and buried Michael's dog tags.

ABOUT THE AUTHOR

Army veteran, Victoria Montes wrote for the Bakersfield Californian.
She won short story contests in The Foreign Service Journals and the Kern
County Writers Festival.
She covered the war in Afghanistan as a photojournalist in 2008.
In film school she produced the short film "A Soldier's Story."

www.ingramcontent.com/pod-product-compliance
Lightning Source LLC
Chambersburg PA
CBHW070332130626
46556CB00007B/2823